Look after me

Look after me

Aoife Walsh

ANDERSEN PRESS

First published in 2014 by
Andersen Press Limited
20 Vauxhall Bridge Road
London SW1V 2SA
www.andersenpress.co.uk

2 4 6 8 10 9 7 5 3 1

British Library Cataloguing in Publication Data available.

ISBN 978 1 849 39713 1

Printed and bound in Great Britain by CPI Group (UK) Ltd, Croydon CR0 4TD

For Pete

Chapter One

It was a wild-feeling day that day. Dad was coming to take us four out for a big walk in it; the two little boys should see some spring before it's over, he said, and we'll run Cal so he stops breaking your mother's heart. It sounded nice, but you could run Cal all the way to Birmingham and he'd still have a tantrum when he got there. Anyway, there were great big sweeps of rain all morning and when Dad finally arrived, late, there was one behind him with the gust of wind that blew him in. When we were kids Mum would drive us out into weather like that; she'd say we should love it or we'd got no blood from her; but we couldn't have taken the wheelchair off-road in the wet, and Cal was screaming, so we went bowling.

Dad looked white, and worried. Feng was excited, he sat waiting patiently while Dad struggled to get bowling shoes onto Cal's feet. Adam and I tried to look like we were enjoying ourselves too, but it was hard for Adam because for years he hasn't enjoyed family outings on purpose. Besides, he hadn't really been speaking to Dad since he'd left. It was different for me, I wasn't exactly angry, it was just that it didn't work – Dad making up for not being there all the time with just a few hours every now and then. But I went where they asked. Adam had only come because Feng asked him. Normally he was good at not doing what other people wanted, but Feng was hard to say no to.

'God! *Bowling*,' Adam muttered to me as he came back from getting a strike, which Dad was trying to clap at the same time as moving the ramp for the little ones to roll their balls down, and holding on to Cal's hood so that he couldn't get into the next lane.

'You used to like it,' I reminded him.

'I used to like a lot of things.' He started warming up like he does, and rocking on his feet, while I was trying to concentrate on my swing. 'What a ludicrous thing to say. I *used* to like being an only child, and Dad reading *Thomas the Tank Engine* to me, and I *used* to like dancing to Destiny's Child songs.'

'Well. Don't brag about it,' I said.

Neither of the little boys wanted to use the ramp, anyway, they said it was for babies. Feng nearly went cross-eyed getting his wheelchair into position. The staff were making a bit of a fuss of him, which is probably what

2

tipped Cal over the edge so that he started bowling everywhere. The guy in the next lane took a ball to the ankle, and there were two big scary bald teenagers on the other side who didn't like it when Cal nipped in ahead of one of them and took his go. Dad was shouting much more than he usually does, especially in public; we never did finish our game.

'I want a Slush Puppy,' Cal said as Dad held him up in the air, away from the bowling balls, and panted. 'Or else I won't go in the car.' He stopped cycling his legs in midair like he was in a cartoon and looked crafty. Adam and I looked at each other because we knew what Mum would say if we brought him back wired with bright blue chemicals. Dad was defiant.

'Of course you can have a Slush Puppy, Cal. Sometimes it's best to just ask, you know, not threaten. You can have one as long as you sit still to drink it, and stop attacking people.' He tries hard with that kind of thing, he calls it positive reinforcement, but I don't know why he bothers because you can see Cal's eyes glazing over the moment he hears that tone in anyone's voice. Adam didn't intervene because of not talking to Dad. Normally he gets bossy in every possible situation, like he's the overlord of our family and responsible for all of us.

So we sat in the café pretending to be a normal family. Perhaps not exactly normal: as well as being in a wheelchair Feng is Chinese, unlike the rest of us; and Cal is tiny with bright red hair, and even when he's still for a second he's coiled like one of those jack-in-the-box toys on a spring. Adam and Dad and I might look more like we belong to each other. We've all got sad pale faces and dirty-brown hair, though Dad is quite thin and I'm not, and Adam has what Dad calls rugby-player shoulders. Though, actually, he'd do anything in the world before he'd play rugby.

What made the whole thing mortifying, because I'm used to it being like that when all of us go out, was that there were some girls from my class at school there too. I'd seen them come in just as we were going to get the drinks, with some boys from the year above, and I'd hoped they'd stay on the lanes, but the girls all showed up in the café and started drinking Diet Cokes and looking at me.

'Who are they?' Adam asked.

I didn't want to make a big deal out of it because he's capable of trying to embarrass me. 'They go to my school.'

'They look interesting,' he said. The other main thing about Adam apart from being bossy, and sarcastic, is that he's a snob about people being clever. He goes to a private school where everyone has to be really smart and he thinks it's a pity that I don't too – so much of a pity that he goes on about it all the time.

'They look nice,' Feng said innocently.

4

Dad started catching up on what we were talking about so I left the table. The good thing about us having only boys in the family then was that at least I could go and hide in the Ladies on my own sometimes. But I met one of the girls from my school in there. Luckily it was Lily Buckley who was the one you wouldn't mind talking to so much.

'Are those all your brothers, Phoebe?' she asked me.

'The big one is,' I said. 'The little ones are my parents' foster kids.' I would have thought she'd have known that they foster, she'd been in my class since primary school, but Mum says people are never thinking about you anywhere near as much as you think they are.

Sure enough it was the vivid colours around Feng's and Cal's that started off that row when we got home, much earlier than Mum wanted us, she said, though she'd been standing at the window looking out for us.

Because they got to shouting straight away, Cal got highly-strung and started tearing round. He sent the little table flying, and the lamp on top of it. Only the light bulb broke but Mum had to stop and take him upstairs, she said not to punish him but to clean him up. Dad wanted to help but she hissed at him, so after he'd been reassuring with Feng and carried him up for his bath he came and sat down on the sofa with me.

I knew Cal would go to sleep. You couldn't get him down for a nap in the afternoon to save your life, but he always did pass out for a while in the evening. Mum said it was normal enough because he was only six. She said most of Cal was because he was tired all the time. Adam said why didn't she just drug him like they used to before we had him, and maybe he'd sleep past five in the morning, and she said but look at him now, it was because no one had ever dealt with him, drugs were just putting it off. Adam said if we put it off for another ten years it wouldn't be our problem anymore.

Dad was pretending to be watching TV, but I knew he wasn't because he wasn't mocking the storylines. Normally you can't concentrate at all when Dad's in the room, wondering what's going to set him off. But I wasn't watching it, either. We were both listening to upstairs. Feng was giggling in the bath and Mum was laughing, so I knew Cal must be asleep already. I could see Adam was listening too; he had his head resting on the arm of the chair so I couldn't see his face, but his ear was standing on end.

The air between us got kind of thick. Adam isn't one to hide what he thinks or even not to be blunt about it. And I could feel Dad feeling guilty, sitting there while Mum was dealing with everything upstairs.

Dad loved Feng and Cal, but I had noticed how all the

arguing, the serious arguing, had kicked off when we got them. A year or so before this, after Feng came, Dad had been trying to persuade Mum to slow down on the fostering for a while. He thought Feng was enough just then, with all the stuff that needed doing to the house as well – we'd never had a kid with physical disabilities before – but then Cal had needed somewhere to go.

I had all kinds of patience with Dad getting tired of everything he had to do and of dealing with the four of us all the time, but I didn't have much with him leaving and leaving Mum to do it on her own. Adam was really angry about it; I'd even noticed him trying to help Mum more, for a while, but that had run down a bit. It was just impossible for him or me to get Cal to do anything. It was frustrating, really, because he'd been with us for nearly a year by then, which was longer than most kids stayed. We'd got used to waving them off, and here was Cal who'd sort of become a fixture, and you kept thinking that he'd settle down a bit but he didn't seem to.

Mum got Feng dressed again and into his room. He had a rest too in the evenings, though he usually read or drew in bed. Then she came downstairs. Dad was meant to stay for dinner but I knew he wouldn't. Saturday used to be the one day we never ate together because everyone had things going on and stuff to do. That had all stopped recently and Dad was supposed to stay, but even if he did they were usually rowing. Right then Mum was livid and she looked like she was going to cry. We went out to the shed.

The shed was mine and Adam's personal space. We were meant to have that in our bedrooms too, but it was hard for Mum to sort out, especially now with Cal who couldn't understand about privacy, Mum said. We have a really big house that we moved into six years ago. 'We'll have to fill it up!' Mum said with her eyes all sparkling, but it turned out that wasn't hard at all.

I'm not really sure if Mum and Dad moved to the big house because they wanted to foster or if they started fostering because they wanted a big house and fostering was a way to fill it up (and pay for it). I was too young before we moved here, only seven, and I don't remember, but I do remember that we used to be a different sort of family. There was just Mum and Dad and Adam and me in a house on a street close into town where all the houses looked the same as ours and had three bedrooms. We were really excited about moving, even though it meant moving schools and longer journeys. Dad said the area was on the up. I think it must have slowed down because it feels just the same as when we moved in. Even the house isn't that different, but it certainly feels fuller.

The shed was already there when we came, and it already wasn't a shed. Dad said once we should call it a summerhouse, and Mum said we could call it that if we liked, and maybe Adam could call it that at school, so we knew she didn't approve of that idea. She hates Adam's school. He got a scholarship to it and between him and Dad they convinced Mum to let him go; well, there was no way Adam wasn't going to go because he's had pretty much a ten-year-plan for his life since he was ten years old, which was just when things were getting chaotic, but Mum can't stand it, she hates private schools. She still watches Adam like a hawk in case he suddenly gets a different accent, and every time she has to go to a parent's evening there she puts on dirty trainers and her sheepskin jacket. She wears nice clothes and make-up to mine.

Anyway, when we moved in the shed hadn't been used for a while by the look of it but it was still OK, with little cupboards and chairs and glass panes in the door. They said it could be a playroom for us where the older kids didn't go. When we were younger Mum and Dad fostered older kids; now we were the older kids, the ones they fostered were younger, and the shed was still ours. Cal wasn't allowed to go there. Mum said it was a shame in some ways because it meant he wasn't allowed in the garden. Our garden's massive; you can't even see the shed from the back door because the garden bends round a corner. But the one time Cal had been in the garden, just after he arrived, he wanted to go in the shed and when Mum told him no he got out later and smashed two of the windows. It hadn't mattered that much yet, him not being allowed in the garden, because we'd only had him since the summer before, which was when he'd been so mental that nothing did matter, and since then it had mostly been winter. Anyway, Cal didn't like outdoors. The lawn's not very smooth and there's no path so Feng didn't go out there, either.

The shed was great as a place to escape, it was always peaceful, but we didn't use to go there all that much in the evenings, even in summer, because there was no TV and no computer. Besides, now that we had younger kids who went to bed earlier, after dark was the time when sometimes it was a bit like it used to be, just the four of us. But since Mum and Dad had started rowing so much, and it was worse once Cal and Feng were in bed, I spent some evenings on my own in there. Adam usually went to his room. He said he didn't trust Cal not to wander in and start throwing his stuff out of the window, if he woke up and got bored. Anyway, he had bags of homework and he needed the computer.

It was only early evening now, and still light, and even though Adam had said he had loads of work to do, going over his exam papers that he'd just finished so he'd be ready to talk about them with his teachers – he works stupidly hard, even Dad tries to get him to ease up sometimes – he wandered down the garden with me. It wasn't raining anymore but there were drops hanging from the ends of all the leaves, and then disappearing in the odd gust of wind that would suddenly blow through you and make you shiver. We could hear Mum shouting. Next thing Cal would be up again. I noticed the curtains were drawn in the shed, which I thought was weird because I'd popped in there that morning to get my grey jumper.

Adam pushed the door open and went in first, which was why he gasped first and jumped back and I shot straight out the door again because I thought he'd seen a man-sized spider or something, but he grabbed my arm and pulled me in. It was very dim. There was someone sitting on the floor against the back wall, which was no less scary than a huge spider right then and my heart was hammering. I might have screamed only Adam had hold of my arm and he said, 'Ssshhh. Don't. It's Leanne.'

I recognised her then. Leanne was the first one Mum and Dad ever fostered. She was a few years older than Adam and we didn't have her for all that long before she went back to her mother. When she was first here I nearly asked Mum and Dad to change their minds because I thought fostering was going to be terrible. Whatever I said she either laughed at or cried, so I hardly ever spoke at all around her. It made me so paranoid and shy that whenever a new kid used to be brought to our house it would take me days to talk to them, because I'd be worried of hurting their feelings somehow or embarrassing them or making them angry. She always called me Fat Phoeb and Phoebeast, and tripped me up and hung around in the hall so she could jump out at me. For years I had to turn on all the lights when I went to the bathroom at night because of her. And she and Mum used to scream at each other, every day, in the morning and at night.

Everyone was sorry when she left, though, except me. Adam even used to email her. For a long time we both did that for some of the kids who left, but they hardly ever wrote back and there was always someone new in the house for us to get used to. I thought it was weird anyway that Adam wanted to keep in touch with Leanne.

Now she was sitting in our shed, so still I thought she was asleep. We went a bit closer and then I saw the light catch her eyes and make them silvery and I saw she was watching us, which made my heart speed right up again.

'What are you doing here?' Adam asked. He'd shut the door and was groping around it behind me for the curtains. I backed away from Leanne towards him.

'Don't pull the curtains,' she said, in a hoarse voice that sounded as if she'd been sitting there in the dark for ages, though it was still light outside and I'd been in there just this morning and it had been empty. 'I don't want anyone to know I'm here.'

'Well, Mum and Dad know we're out here and they'd think it was odd if we were sitting in the dark,' Adam said, though he stopped with his hand on the curtains. 'Anyway, you can't see the shed from our house.'

'You can from upstairs,' Leanne said, which was true. 'Put the lamp on.'

Light flooded the shed suddenly, and even though we'd only been in there a few seconds I half-shut my eyes. Adam was blinking, but Leanne stared straight at us. She was all wrapped up in a big coat, though it was practically summer and we'd even put the heater away in a cupboard. There was something on the floor beside her. She was holding her hand over part of it.

'What the bloody hell is that?' Adam asked, his voice rising as if he was scared.

'Baby,' Leanne said.

'What?' Adam shot forward but I stayed where I was. It *was* a baby, too. It was all wrapped up in a blanket, like pictures of baby Jesus I used to draw when I was little. It was asleep.

'Is it yours?' he asked her, looking down at them. She shrugged. I didn't know what to do. I didn't know anything about people having babies, except how it works, with their bodies and stuff, the basic things. 'Is it, Leanne?'

'I had it,' she said. 'But I don't want it. That's why I brought it here.'

'What?'

'Is it new?' I asked. I had to go a bit closer to have a look. You couldn't see much except blanket.

'You didn't have it here, did you?' Adam sounded really scared now. He was looking round, for bloodstains or mess, I suppose, but the shed looked just the same except for Leanne and the baby itself.

Leanne laughed, which made me remember her living with us even more. 'You're a cretin, Adam. I had her a week ago. Two weeks ago. I wouldn't be sitting around here if I'd just pushed her out.'

'Why did you bring her here?' he asked, kneeling down beside the baby.

Leanne shrugged again. 'I don't want her. I haven't been well and I can't look after her. So it was either leave her in a phone box or come here, and they've boarded up all the phone boxes.'

'Why here?' I went and sat down near Adam. He kept looking from Leanne to the baby. I just looked at Leanne. She looked just the same age, or even a bit younger. When she lived with us she'd seemed practically grown up. I suppose I must have got a lot older in the meantime. Her face was puffy, which I might have thought was having had a baby recently, except that there were finger marks in the puffiness and a purple patch at the bottom of her neck.

'I can't look after her,' Leanne said flatly, 'but I don't want her to go into Care.'

'Why did you have her, then?' Adam sounded mystified.

Leanne looked at me, almost rolled her eyes, as if it was me and her against the stupidity of all males. She must have noticed I was older too. She used to treat me like a toddler.

'I thought I was going to have help,' she said finally, 'but I don't. As it turns out.'

'Mum will help you,' I said unwillingly. I didn't want Leanne back. I didn't want her back at all. Things were hard enough. But there was the baby, not to mention the bruises.

'I don't want help. It might be hard for you to believe, with your bloody smiley parents and your big eyes, but I don't actually want her.' She wiped her nose on the back of her arm. 'I would have left her on a step, only I don't want her in Care, like I said. Then I thought of here, I thought here wouldn't be too bad. It was the best place I ever lived. Your parents are all right. They'll look after her, she'll have a family.'

I opened my mouth to tell her Dad wasn't living with us at the moment, but Adam said over the top, 'You're going to leave her here?'

'Yeah. I don't want anything more to do with it.'

'But they'll come looking for you!' I said.

'They won't.'

'Don't be daft,' Adam said. 'Of course they will. You can give her up for adoption, or whatever, but they'll have to do all that interviewing you and stuff first.'

'No. They don't know she's mine. No one knows she exists yet.'

'No one? What about at the hospital?'

'I didn't have her at the hospital. And this is exactly why. No bloody social workers yet, not till I'm well out the way. Don't look at me like that, you,' she said to me. 'You know nothing.'

'I know they'll be after you,' I said. 'And what are we supposed to do with her?'

'Wait a bit, Fat Phoeb, then take her to your Mum and Dad,' she said. 'They'll know. Only don't say it was me.'

'Why shouldn't we?' I said.

'Why would you? Don't you think she'll be better off without me?' she asked, and I did, after all, not that I thought we would really be able to keep it a secret who the mother was.

'But you . . .' Adam hesitated. 'Are you going to be OK?'

'I'm going to be fine, I'm going to be on my own and I can look after myself. And she'll be fine with you. Just say you found her left here. I've got her clothes, too.' She pulled a carrier bag out from under the chair behind her and held it against her chest for a moment. 'They'll keep her, your mum and dad, won't they?'

I was going to tell her again about Dad moving out, but again Adam spoke over the top of me. 'They'll try, anyway. Mum loves babies. She'll say this was Fate.'

Leanne got up, all stiff from sitting too long on the floor, and dumped the bag on the red chair. 'Give me a couple of hours' head start before you take her in,' she said. 'Can you do that?'

Adam said yes just as I was thinking no.

'If she cries there's a bottle in there, and a carton of milk. She doesn't drink that much.' She didn't look at the baby or anything but she bent down and touched it on the blanket over its tummy. Then she was gone and there was just Adam and me looking at each other over the baby.

Chapter Two

'So now what are we going to do?' I asked him.

'We'll just stay here for a bit.'

'We can't just stay here. We haven't even had dinner yet, Adam.'

'We'll manage something. You can go in and I'll stay here. Tell Mum I want some time on my own.' He grinned. 'You can bring me some dinner out.'

'It's not funny, Adam,' I said, shocked. 'This is serious.'

'I know.'

'Why didn't you tell Leanne Dad's left?'

'Oh, we'll manage fine without Dad; like he'd make any difference. Anyway he hasn't *left*. Not for good.' He saw my face. 'Look, until they get the stones to tell us he's gone and that's it, I'm not even going to try and deal with their mess, OK? Because God knows there's going to be enough of it then.'

'OK, so it's not final yet, but Mum's not going to be allowed to keep a baby, is she, when Dad's moved out?'

'Probably not. But look, I don't know how Leanne would've reacted if we had told her, she might have gone off with the baby then and, well, who knows what she'd have done. It *obviously* wasn't a good situation where they were.'

'No,' I said. I was uncomfortable. 'Did you see Leanne's . . .'

'Leanne's not our problem, Phoebe, she didn't want us to help her. She said she needed us to take the baby and then she could sort herself out. Anyway, one thing at a time.'

'I suppose,' I said doubtfully. 'So are we really not going to tell Mum whose it is?'

'No.'

'You think no?'

'We're not going to tell Mum at all.'

Then I had to sit back on my heels and let him tell me what he was thinking because I couldn't say it for him, even though I knew, really. And I probably knew even then I'd do it because I always do what Adam wants. He's always so convinced himself that he knows what's best, even when it goes against what any normal person would think, that he convinces me too.

He wanted us to keep the baby. In the shed. Not say

19

anything to anyone at all but look after her for a while. 'Just a little while, Phoebe.' Mum was completely stressed out and it was the wrong time, just now, to bring a baby into the mix. We should keep her out of it as long as we possibly could, at least till Mum was feeling better or things were more sorted or even till Dad came back; then we could tell them and maybe there'd be a chance we could hang on to her, and by then we'd all be in a position to think what to do about Leanne as well.

I thought it was crazy, not because I couldn't see the point in it because I could. I didn't want to put a baby in Care either. We'd seen how kids were sometimes when they'd been in the system for ages. But it wouldn't be our fault if that happened; we'd had it drummed into us that stuff like that is completely out of our hands, even mostly out of Mum and Dad's hands. And things were so up in the air. I still hoped Dad was coming home one day but we couldn't know what was going to happen about that, and I didn't really think we'd have got to keep her anyway, even if everything was great and Dad had never left. I knew it didn't work like that, all neat. And it wasn't as if Mum and Dad didn't have their hands full with the four of us before he left. But the craziest thing of all was thinking we could keep a baby in the shed without anyone knowing. I know it's our private space but it's only at the bottom of the garden and we didn't know anything about babies. We'd never had one. Mum said it wouldn't be fair to us, we'd all get too attached. 'When you're grown up, maybe,' she'd always said with a sad smile. 'Maybe that's when we'll get a baby.'

'Anyway,' I said to Adam, 'we've got to go to school. It's not a dog, we can't tie it up and leave it on its own.'

He didn't want to listen to that, he was looking at the baby. She was stirring a bit. The blanket fell away from her face some more so we could see her better. Her eyelids were fluttering. 'I'd better get the bottle sorted in case she screams,' he said. 'You be ready to grab her.'

'I don't want to grab her.'

He was rooting through the bag Leanne had left and came up with a baby bottle and a little carton of special milk, about half a pint it looked like. 'Have we got any scissors in here?'

'You can tear it, can't you?'

'How much do you think she'll drink?' He held the bottle up to the light. It had measurements on the side.

'I don't know. Fill it up, I suppose.'

'Maybe it says here.' The carton had writing all over.

Just then we heard Mum shouting for us. She must have been standing right at the back door. I jumped up. The baby gave a little whimper and started turning her head from side to side.

'Don't tell her,' Adam said urgently.

'It's not going to work. We don't know anything, we can't do this. She's too small, and babies are hard, everyone says so, even for parents.'

'Just don't tell her yet. Let's see, just for a bit, just for tonight. Mum's had a crap day, she's not exactly going to take it calmly now.'

'OK,' I said, after a bit, watching him pour half the carton into the bottle all splashily. He put it down and kneeled over the baby, then looked up at me.

'Can you pass her to me?'

I didn't know how to pick her up either. I'd held a baby before, my friend Marika's little brother years ago, but their mum had just put him in my arms. Adam had settled himself in the chair with the bottle and was shifting his arms up and down experimentally. He looked at me again. 'Come on, Phoebe, or Mum'll be out here.'

I bent down and sort of scooped the baby up. I knew I had to put a hand under her head, but even though she was so little there seemed to be too much of her to hold on just the other hand. I got her into Adam's arms as quick as I could. There was a bit of a jolt and she started really crying. Mum was calling again and I knew if we could hear her she could probably hear a crying baby, or would if she listened, so I ran out, opening and shutting the door as quick as I could to keep the noise in.

***

22

The garden was beginning to get dark now because no one ever trims the top of our trees or hedges; there were deep twilight shadows at the edges under the walls, and a channel up the middle of lighter gloom. It looked longer than usual. I could hear the thin crying, though it stopped as I ran round the corner; I hoped she'd really finished, but either way Mum hadn't heard her – the back door was open but she wasn't there.

It was warm as I went in. Mum was sitting at the big round table in the little room she won't let us call the dining room – it's just the little room. It's barely separate from the kitchen, anyway. Her head was bowed as if she was praying, but she was just waiting. Feng was there too. Cal was standing up next to his chair. His eyes were glittering, like they do when people have been arguing. There were plates of food set out for me and Adam. Mum looked up at me. 'Have you washed your hands? Where's your brother?'

'He said he wanted to be on his own for a bit. He said he'd eat later,' I muttered. I slid into my chair.

'Oh. Well, fair enough.' She picked up her fork. 'Bless us, O Lord, and these thy gifts, which through thy bounty we are about to receive, through Christ our Lord. Amen. Your dad had to go.'

'Oh.'

'He said he'd see you Monday.' She put so much pasta

in her mouth she couldn't talk. My mouth was too full as well. Cal was looking at the ceiling, probably wondering if he could reach it with a forkful of spaghetti. Feng was still trying to twiddle his round his fork. I reached over to help him, so that Mum could get her dinner eaten quickly and be ready to grab Cal; if you don't catch him as soon as he's finished he runs round the house rubbing his saucey hands on the wall and dropping spaghetti on the floor.

'It's really nice, Gillian,' Feng ventured.

'Oh, good.'

He started telling me all about his school project on the Great Fire of London. Because Feng was only eight, when he rattled on sometimes you might think he wasn't picking up on the vibes around him, but actually he was well tuned in on it all. I think he probably just didn't get fed up as easily as the rest of us, so he would actually try to fix an atmosphere rather than waiting for it to be over.

After dinner I had to help Mum clean up. Feng and Cal liked to watch *Total Wipeout* on the TV. It kept Cal quiet, or at least in one room. I started scraping plates while she ran a sink full of water for the saucepot and the bits and pieces, like the beakers we drink from when Cal's around. Adam's plate was still sitting on the table, though Cal had tried to tip it over. 'Shall I take it out to him?' I said, all casual.

Mum looked over at me quietly. 'I thought he wanted

alone time?' I shrugged. 'All right, love, if you think. Is he OK?'

'Yeah, he's OK.'

'I'm sorry about the argument.'

'Mmmm,' I said.

'I know I say it all the time. Things will get better, you know that, don't you?'

'Yeah.'

'There are always hard times. Some times are so hard you don't know how you'll get through them, but you do.' I didn't say anything. 'Is Adam upset about it?'

'How would I know?'

'True.' She pulled her rubber gloves off. 'You can always talk to me, you know that.'

'Yeah, of course.'

'Because I know we haven't talked that much about things, since your dad moved out.' She watched me. 'Things are so up in the air at the moment, for me too, and him, but if you want to talk I want to as well. Even if I don't have the answers yet.'

'I know.'

'Or – to your dad. Or to both of us. We both think you're pretty amazing you know, the way you take things in your stride and just get on with them, but if you're ever not taking them in your stride...'

'I know.'

'I must say it to Adam too. Not that I'll get anything out of him, control freak that he is. Go on, then, take that out to his lordship.'

The yellow light from the kitchen followed me all the way up to the garden corner. I could hear Mum singing in the kitchen too as she scrubbed the saucepot – '*Too late my brothers, too late, but never mind...*' and Cal yelling at her all the way from the front room to shut up, but she carried on singing. Round the corner the garden was all the darker, so what showed up was the light in the shed gleaming at the edge of the blind.

Adam was sitting on the edge of the red chair, which has busted springs so it sags right down if you sit back in it, with his knees squished together like a little kid needing the toilet. He had the baby balanced on one arm and the other hand holding the bottle, hovering above her face as if he was ready to stuff it in her mouth as soon as she opened it. As a matter of fact it was a little bit open. I crept round behind him to have a look, and she was awake. She was looking at something just in front of her crossed dark eyes.

'She's been awake since you left,' Adam whispered.

'Did she have all that milk?'

'No, hardly any.' He tilted it upright to show me. 'But I looked at the carton and it says babies under two weeks are only meant to drink 100 mil in a go and she's had about that. I think. Maybe a bit less.'

'Oh, yeah? That's not much, is it?' I said doubtfully, looking at the scale on the side of the bottle. 'She didn't want any more?'

'No. After two weeks they're meant to have a bit more in a go. Like 130 mil.'

We looked at each other. 'Do we definitely know she's under two weeks?'

'I think that's what Leanne said.'

'But Leanne sort of seemed like she didn't know which end was up, didn't she.'

'Now you mention it, yeah. She's very small, though, isn't she?'

'But I think babies come in different sizes.' She almost seemed to be looking at me. 'She's a bit yellow.'

'Aren't they always that colour?'

I shrugged. 'How often does she have to feed?'

'Well, that's the problem. Six times, it says on the carton. In a day, like in twenty-four hours.'

'Why's that a problem?'

'Well, you're not supposed to keep the milk once she's drunk some of it; you're meant to chuck it out after two hours.'

'So we chuck this out and keep the rest of the carton till the next feed?'

'Yes, only you're meant to sterilise the bottle in between.'

'How...?'

'We'll have to find out. But now I think she might need changing. Her nappy, I mean,' Adam said uneasily. 'She smells strange.'

'You mean like poo?' I'd been a bit squeamish talking about poo when I was younger, but having Feng and Cal around meant I'd got over it.

'No. She smells of vinegar.'

'I can't stay out too long or Mum will notice. So let's do it now.'

We got her on to the floor and unrolled the blanket. She only had a vest on underneath, one of those ones that button between the legs. 'Should she not have more on than that?' I asked, shocked. It suddenly felt really cold in the shed.

'She's been in the blanket,' Adam said doubtfully. 'Dig the heater out, Phoebe.' He flipped the blanket back over her while I opened the little cupboard and poked around in it. We'd only put the heater away a couple of weeks before so it wasn't too cobwebby. I plugged it in and switched it on. It makes a bit of a noise but it's quite good.

Adam bravely unpopped the vest and rolled it up a bit while I had a look in the bag for nappies. There were only four, and not many clothes, just a yellow vest and a white one with pink flowers, and a pair of jeans that were tiny but looked too big, and one of those suits that are a top and a bottom in one. I thought we'd better put that on her too, if we could manage it. There was a little yellow hat as well. Adam reached past me for one of the nappies. 'Now we just have to figure out how to put this on,' he said.

'Should we not wash her first?' I asked. We looked at each other, and at the baby, who didn't look too pleased.

'We can't,' he said firmly after a moment, 'we haven't got any water.'

'No. Has it occurred to you how we're going to manage without any water?'

'There's the garden tap,' he said, holding up the nappy to figure it out. He seemed quite happy. 'But it'll be too cold to wash her with.'

'Yes. Too cold to do anything with.'

'Maybe we can heat some up with the heater later on.'

'That'll take for ever.'

'Or – I know – we can get a kettle.'

'What with? Have you got any money?'

'Dad gave me a tenner today.'

'Me too, but we'd have to buy nappies, and milk and stuff.'

'Maybe we can ask Mum for one. Say we want to be able to make tea down here.' He had figured out which side was the back of the nappy and eased it under her.

Now he folded up the front and stuck down the tabs. 'There! Easy. You can do the next one.'

'Thanks very much. Now what are we going to do with her tonight?'

'I think we should both sleep out here. After this we can take it in turns...'

'We're so going to have to tell Mum tomorrow. If we make it till then.'

'...But for the first night I think we should both be here.'

I stared at him. 'How can we? Mum's not going to say, "All right, you sleep outside every night even though you've never done it before."'

'I can get out my window after I've gone to bed and climb down the tree. No, look, I can, it's easy.'

'What about me?'

'You can too. You'll have to.'

'No way. I'm too fat.'

'Don't be silly, Phoebe. This is the way I see it: you go in now, and you can Google some stuff about babies so we know the basics, like how you sterilise bottles. And try to figure out what we'll need. Tomorrow one of us can go shopping. Then after a bit you say you're going to bed. Get yourself a sleeping bag, and bring another blanket for the baby, maybe, in case it gets cold, and go through my room and climb down the tree. Then, once you're here, I'll go in the house, so Mum knows I'm in, then I'll climb out and everyone's happy.'

'Don't you think Mum might notice quite quickly if she only ever sees one of us at a time?'

'She's not noticing anything at the moment,' he said.

'What if she secretly checks on us in our rooms after we're asleep?'

'Why would she?'

'I don't know. It seems quite a motherly thing to do. Maybe she does it every night.'

'Well. We'll find out tonight, won't we?'

Chapter Three

Mum was lying on the sofa in the front room when I went in. She was on her back with her eyes shut. I'd have thought she was asleep but it was only about nine o'clock, although I couldn't hear any racket anywhere. 'Mum?' I whispered.

'Yes, love?' she said without opening her eyes.

'Where's Cal?'

'Hopefully drowning in the bath,' she said.

Now that she said it I could hear splashing. The big bathroom is just at the top of the stairs. There's another one, a little one, just between Cal's and Feng's rooms, but we'd learned a bigger space was always better for Cal. We needed it for Feng too; Dad had fitted it up with bars and things so he could move about and not slip.

'He does like water, doesn't he?' You wouldn't leave Cal anywhere else on his own, but he nearly always gets really calm in the bath, he loves it.

'Yes.' Mum opened her eyes and turned over towards me. 'Maybe that's what's wrong with him, do you think? Maybe his natural habitat is water, and having to be on land instead just drives him mad.'

'Would that make him more or less evolved than most people?' I asked. The computer was in the corner of the room, on the little desk near the window. We're not allowed to have wireless Internet in case we get a kid who looks at stuff they shouldn't.

Mum kind of snorted a laugh. 'Do you two still hate Cal?'

'We don't *hate* him,' I said.

'No.'

She was waiting for me to say more. I said, 'He doesn't get much easier, though, does he?'

'No.' She sighed. 'I don't suppose it's great for him, at the moment. One of these days we might have to decide whether it's making him more or less secure, being here.'

'What?' I said.

'Sorry, darling. I wasn't really talking to you. I don't suppose I meant it, either. Sorry. It's not having Dad here to talk to. I'm very, very thankful for you, do you know that?'

'Can I use the computer?'

'Feng's waiting for you to read him a story. Are you too busy?'

'Oh, God.' I'd forgotten. I'd taken lately to reading to Feng at bedtime, because last holidays I'd started helping him learn to read, and so me reading proper books to him was like a reward. It was nice, going through all my favourites with him. It meant Mum could concentrate on Cal for a bit too.

'It's all right, you've got exams coming up. I'll do it.'

I went out into the hall and shouted up the stairs, 'Feng?'

'I've got the book,' he shouted from his bedroom. We were reading *George's Marvellous Medicine*.

'Is it OK if Mum reads to you tonight? I've got to revise.'

'OK.' He sounded cheerful anyway. Mum got up and gave me a kiss on the way out.

I sat down and switched the computer on. I didn't really know where to start, there were so many questions. I started with 'how do you sterilise bottles' and went on to 'how much should a two-weeks-old baby weigh'. Adam should have been doing it, really. I'm not at my best with computers, or spelling. They used to think I was dyslexic at school when I was little, but only because they compared me to Adam. Mum and Dad knew I wasn't because Dad's dyslexic himself. I do all right but I have to work quite hard. Adam could coast right through if he wanted and still get brilliant marks, but that doesn't stop him slaving.

There's always loads of paper and some pens on the desk, though lots of it has scribble on it. Cal's not meant to use it but it's hard to keep him away, and Dad says at least if he's destroying paper he's not head butting the computer.

Actually he's really good with computers and he loves them, but he has to have someone sitting with him in case he gets in a temper.

I had to write loads of stuff down or I knew I'd never remember it, and even if I did Adam wouldn't believe me. Like if I told him how many vests you were supposed to have for a new baby. I must have been there for quite a while because Mum came back down after she'd got the boys to sleep and I was still tap-tapping away.

'What are you doing?' she asked, sitting down. 'Homework?'

'Yeah.'

'What subject?'

'English,' I said straight away, because English always takes the longest on the computer, and then I thought how tired I was of reading through loads and loads of pages of grown-ups wailing about their babies, so I said, 'and science. What are babies meant to wear?'

She laughed and said, 'What's that for?'

'Science. It's a new project, about looking after babies, you know.'

'Oh yes,' she said, interested. 'When Caitlin was here she did something like that, do you remember? Are you going to have one of those crying dolls too?'

'Don't know,' I said. I did remember that doll. It used to cry all night.

'But you've only got one week before exams. Surely you're not starting a new project now, are you?'

'Oh, yeah, well; Mr Brundage said we won't really be doing it till after exams, but he gave us all a few questions each, you know, to start us thinking about it. So that we're ready to start. Afterwards.'

'It seems a bit harsh to expect you to think about that right when you've got to be revising.'

'Well, you know Mr Brundage. But it's only a few questions. So what do babies wear?' I said hopefully.

'It depends on the time of year, I suppose.'

'Well, what about summer? Like now?'

'Would you call this summer?' she asked dreamily. She was stroking the sofa, which is made out of big corduroy and feels smooth where it's worn on the arms.

'What, Mum?'

'Oh, a vest and a sleepsuit I suppose.'

'What's a sleepsuit? One of those things with feet?'

'Yes, that's right. Or a vest and a little outfit, like a T-shirt and trousers, or a dress and tights. It's different when it's hot. You've got to be careful not to let babies heat up too much.'

I'd picked that up already, from Google. 'What do you call it when they're all yellow?' I asked.

'Jaundice? Adam had that. He had to go back into hospital the day after we came home, it was awful.'

'Hospital?'

'Yes. They put him under a sunlamp. Light's the thing, light and feeding them loads. That's how they get it, not feeding enough so that they're not weeing enough – they fill up with urea. I think that's right, anyway. You'd better look it up if you want to be sure.'

'How yellow was Adam?' I asked casually.

'Oh, very. You could tell straight away. Even the whites of his eyes were yellow. Don't you think you've been working long enough now?'

'Yeah,' I said, and quickly cleared the history box before I shut the computer down. 'I'm going to go to bed now, I think. Er – has Adam come in?'

'Not yet,' she said absently, taking a book off the bookshelf.

The sleeping bags were in the cupboard under the stairs, and way at the back there were some blankets. There weren't any of those with holes in like the pink one the baby was wrapped in, the kind babies always have, and most of them felt much too heavy and stiff and scratchy somehow, but I did find a nice soft fleecy checked one that we used to use for picnics, so I pulled that out. I went in the bathroom too and got a whole load of cotton wool. We never seem to use it much so it had been sitting there for ages but it was in a bag and it looked clean. I put it in the jug Mum used for washing Cal's hair because if you got the showerhead down while he was in the bath he flooded the whole floor. I'd read that you were supposed to have muslin cloths, but I didn't know what they were, so I got two bath towels and a tea towel from downstairs, and one of Feng's flannels, and a pillowcase, and hoped something would do. If nothing else we could make a sort of bed for her. She'd been lying on an old pillow we had out there, but I'd read enough already to know that wasn't right. It wasn't very clean either.

Then I went in my room and emptied out my school bag and put everything in it, except the blanket which wouldn't fit, and all the notes I'd made as well, and stuck my head out the door. I could hear the music Mum was listening to downstairs but nothing else, so I shut my door and scurried into Adam's room and shut his door too, and went over and opened the window.

The tree grows right up against the window. We've never been big tree climbers but I did remember Adam climbing up to the window from the ground, and down again, soon after we moved in, just to prove it could be done. I don't like heights much. I knew I couldn't get myself out the window with the bag and the blanket, so I threw the blanket down. It got stuck on a branch halfway but I'd be passing it so I could get it on the way. Then I put the bag on my shoulders and got up so I was kneeling on the window sill with my head practically on the branch. It was only a step across. It was a big strong branch too.

There wasn't any other way to get out without Mum hearing me; I stayed hunched there thinking about it. I might never have done it but I knew how impatient Adam would be, waiting for me. I knew Mum would be waiting for him, downstairs, too, and I knew he couldn't come in till I got to the shed because he couldn't leave the baby on her own. I stood up and reached over, clung on to the branch above and stepped across with one foot. Then I was straddling space for a while before I managed to move the other one.

That was the hardest part, actually. Even when I got a branch caught up in the back of my jumper it wasn't too bad, because I was nearly down by then, so when I toppled forward it wasn't too scary. I even grabbed the blanket with one hand as I landed.

The baby was asleep again when I got there. I think Adam might have been as well, in the chair. I didn't think she was that yellow, though I was keen to get a look at her eyes when she opened them, but she didn't look too good, she was all sort of huddled looking and her hair was flattened down on her head and she had sick marks on her chin, and the blanket was a bit wet where she'd had the bottle. So was her vest, underneath, and she definitely smelled funny.

Because she was asleep we decided Adam should go in and say goodnight to Mum and get his stuff before we tried to clean her up. So I took her from him and he stood up and then he took her back and let me sit down and arrange myself a bit and then passed her to me. He took the bottle in with him. He was going to clean it up properly with hot water and stuff. I'd told him I didn't think we could possibly sterilise it without special stuff and without Mum noticing, so we'd just have to take a chance till tomorrow.

When he was gone I sat all still for a while, but the baby didn't move so eventually I settled back a bit. I decided she should definitely be wearing more clothes, because it was feeling colder and colder behind the sort of layer of heat the heater made. Till Adam was back to help I hugged the blanket around her a bit more. Then she sort of squirmed and her hand came out and touched mine, and it felt really chilly. I could reach the fleecy blanket with my toe, so I dragged it over with my foot and shunted around a bit till I could pick it up and spread it over both of us. It still had twigs on it from getting caught in the tree but it made us nice and warm. I wished I could be in my cosy bedroom though. It was funny to think there would only be three people in the whole house tonight. Of course it had felt quite empty since Dad moved out anyway; I thought of him in his new scruffy flat that I'd only seen once and which wasn't all that much better than the shed, actually. We weren't the only ones sleeping somewhere else.

The baby wasn't heavy but holding her in the same position was making my back ache, so I shifted her up a bit till the arm holding her head was propped on the arm of the chair. I could feel her breathing, her chest going up and down, and her little legs with the feet crossed against my other wrist. I suppose she hadn't stretched out yet. I've seen pictures of babies inside their mothers, they're all curled up in a ball almost. Upside down too, which you wouldn't think would be very comfortable. She was really tiny; I could easily close my fingers around her knee, and the bones felt very fragile.

Then she gave a sort of wriggle and opened her eyes and looked at me. I'd been thinking that it was lucky she hadn't cried much yet, but now she gave a sort of a whimper and her chin started shaking. She had a very little pointy chin. I was scared I wouldn't be able to stop her if she really cried, so I rocked her and sang. Mum sings all the time, but the only song I could think of right then was 'Twinkle Twinkle Little Star', so I sang that over and over and she didn't cry. I thought she must be pretty scared. Even if she couldn't see me properly I wouldn't feel like Leanne, or like whoever else she'd been with before. She might be able to tell that I didn't know how to look after her properly and I couldn't even sterilise her bottle for her. That's when I thought, we really had to tell Mum. I nearly got up and took her in to the house then, because I realised, this was a real baby, a person nearly, and we didn't know what to do at all and if we messed it up it would be really bad. But I was afraid to get out of the chair in case I got tangled in the blanket or lost my balance or dropped her, so I waited for Adam to get back.

He was beaming when he came in, with his sleeping bag and his school bag too. 'Everyone's in bed,' he said. 'I brought you a Kit Kat. And, look!' He'd found the old thermos that Mum used to have when she was little, which we always took on picnics when it was cold, and filled it up with boiling water. When he took a look at me I think he knew what I was going to say, so he unwrapped the Kit Kat and broke it in half and gave me a bit. Then he said it was time to clean her up, so he took the jug and went outside to get some water from the garden tap.

'You can't put that cold water on her,' I said. I'd finished the Kit Kat.

'Don't have to, look.' He poured some of the hot water in from the thermos flask and splashed it around with his hand. 'Lovely. I tell you, if we get a kettle tomorrow we'll have no problems.'

'We can't just get a kettle,' I said grumpily, sitting up a bit. My back hurt again. 'They're really expensive and we'd have to get loads of other stuff too, nappies and more

42

bottles and stuff to sterilise them, and milk. And we've got no fridge to put milk in, or anything.'

'It's not like it's boiling hot, and if the cartons aren't open they'll last days. Easily. We'll manage.' He saw my face. 'Please, Phoebe. Let's just try for tonight, anyway. If we can't do it we can't, but let's give it a try. Look, we might be rookies but we're her best hope at the moment.'

'But she's going to want another feed, and what if we run out of milk? And we can't even sterilise the bottle, what if we make her sick?'

'We won't make her sick. I scrubbed that bottle in really hot water and then I sprayed it all with the stuff Mum soaks Feng's things in and scrubbed it again, and then I put water in and stuck it in the microwave. It's clean. And we won't run out of milk, she's only little. She doesn't need much.'

That was the thing, reading about babies on the Internet had made me feel like babies did need much, that they needed absolutely tons of things, as well as people looking after them who knew what to do and would still know what to do if something went wrong, but Adam hadn't read that stuff and he didn't think so. And it was true that Mum was just at the top of the garden if something terrible happened. So I said OK.

Chapter Four

After Adam had got the water ready he spread out one of the towels I'd brought and put the pile of cotton wool next to it. It was so complicated, trying to get her lying down without either of us dropping her, and stripping her without freezing her, and then I was afraid to take the nappy off so Adam shunted me out of the way and he did it. He's always less afraid than me of getting things wrong. He washed her with cotton wool, with me telling him from the side how you had to be careful to dry babies properly. At least the tumble dryer was working so the towel was soft instead of scratchy. We thought Leanne might not have kept her very clean because she was such a mess, and her vest was damp now anyway, so we washed her all over. She didn't like the vest going over her face one bit. We didn't know what to use to wash her and just tried sprinkling the warm water on her, but we ended up cleaning her head with the flannel I'd brought because her hair was so sticky, and then I used it on her hands too. We didn't use any soap because if we'd put soap in the water we'd have had to rinse her with different water and we thought we might run out of the hot stuff. Anyway it might have got in her eyes. Cal makes enough of a racket if he gets soap in his eyes, I didn't want to see what a baby might do.

Adam put her nappy on and then the yellow vest, but he made me put the sleepsuit on because I knew what it was. It took ages to do up because there were so many poppers and I kept doing them wrong, but in the end it was done and I lifted her up and put her on the blanket which Adam had spread out so I could wrap her in it and stand up with her. Adam had got the bottle ready and sat down so I passed her to him, and then got the tea towel from the pile of things we'd brought out and tucked it under her chin so her clothes wouldn't get wet.

'She needs some bibs,' I said.

'Maybe we can nick some of Feng's tomorrow,' he said. Feng used to have to wear bibs because he found it hard to use his fork properly.

'Don't be stupid, they'd be massive. She'd fall through the neck hole.'

'We'll have to buy some then.'

'What with?'

'Moneyboxes,' he said. We did have moneyboxes. Dad said we should have savings accounts but Mum said moneyboxes were good enough until we were old enough to need credit cards, and Adam backed her up because he likes to have his stuff where he can see it, and you can't get money out of savings accounts for days and days. We were meant to be saving up for holidays, but we didn't even know if we'd be going anywhere yet, with Mum and Dad not speaking much. It would probably be enough for a while, though I knew I didn't have all that much and I doubted if Adam did. He didn't have a job or anything. If there was something he really wanted he asked for it for his birthday or Christmas. His Christmas list was always very specific.

'We'll have to buy her some clothes, though,' I said. 'These aren't anywhere near enough.'

'Really?' he asked, not very interested. He was watching the baby.

'Of course they're not. Even the vests aren't enough, she's only got one clean one now. And how are we going to wash them?'

'We'll think of something.'

I sat down in the other chair and watched too. The baby was drinking her milk. Her hair was all fluffy now. It was dark brown, not like Leanne's. She didn't have much but it looked like those fluffy little feathers you find sometimes in the park.

'The loft,' I said suddenly. 'Mum's got some of our old baby clothes in there.'

'Oh good.'

'I'll have a look tomorrow morning.'

'Good idea. You can get back in early before anyone's up and check out the loft, and then we'll know what we need before you go shopping.'

'Me go shopping? Why not you?'

'You're a girl. It'll look less weird for you to be buying nappies.'

I thought that was probably right, actually. Anyway, I wasn't keen to be left on my own with the baby for long, though I knew I'd have to be if we were really going to do this. Mum, and even Dad, would notice if Adam just disappeared and never turned up even for meals. That made me remember something.

'Aren't you supposed to be going swimming with Mum tomorrow?' I asked.

'No,' he said. 'There was a change of plan. She asked Stephen to go instead.'

Mum and Dad always used to take Feng and Cal to the swimming pool every weekend. It was great because the pool was opened specially on Sunday mornings only for disabled kids and their families, so it was good for Feng, but also for Cal. He loves the swimming pool and it really tires him out and if ever we missed a Sunday swim he would be much worse all week. It was too difficult to take him just at normal opening hours. If the pool and the changing rooms were packed like ordinary and he got into a tantrum it was just awful. Even on Sunday mornings it took two people to look after him and Feng and get them changed and all that, and Mum and Dad wouldn't go together now. For the last two weeks Dad had taken them, and Adam went with him one week and I went the other, but Dad had a shift at work this week so Mum had to go. I knew she wasn't happy about Adam going with her, or me either. She would have loved it if she could think of something that we'd all enjoy doing together, but she had a thing about not cutting too much into our weekends with things that were too blatantly for Feng and Cal; she said it wasn't us who were the foster carers, and she especially worried about it around then because we had exams, and the end-of-year play and all that stuff. So she must have asked Stephen, who's one of the social workers. They do things like that sometimes, but it was bad news, because she must have told him about Dad moving out.

'I know,' said Adam grimly. 'But she said they had to let them know anyway. She said they had no choice. You know Mum and the truth.'

I was cold again and I got up to unroll my sleeping bag. The shed floor is just painted planks and quite hard but we did have a rug. I hadn't brought any pyjamas. I got in the bag and lay down and watched them for a while. The baby had gone to sleep with the bottle still in her mouth. 'Are you going to hold her all night?'

'No, I'll put her down on that big blanket. Can you fold it up a bit for me? But she hasn't drunk all this milk yet. I might jiggle her a bit if she doesn't wake up soon. We don't want to waste it, there's only a couple more lots left in the carton.'

I had folded up the blanket without getting out of my bag. 'I don't think we can do this, Adam.'

'You keep saying that but we've managed so far. She's clean now. She's asleep, she's fine. She hasn't even cried that much.'

'We've only had her four hours. And everyone knows babies get much worse at night.'

'Well, like I said, if she does and we can't cope we've only got to take her up the garden. Go to sleep if you want.'

'And we'll definitely tell Mum tomorrow if it's too rough tonight?'

'If we think we can't handle it.'

'What about if *I* think we can't handle it?' I watched them for a bit again. 'If Dad doesn't come back, do you think they'll take Feng and Cal away?'

He didn't even look over at me, just set the bottle down and started to jog his knee about just a little bit. 'No.'

***

49

As a matter of fact the baby didn't cry all that much more at night, though it was enough. I went to sleep after that, I was really tired, but of course it wasn't all that comfortable on the floor, or with the lamp on, and I woke up a bit when Adam was putting the baby down on the blanket. She didn't wake up though, and he got his sleeping bag and lay down the other side so she was in between us, and I went back to sleep. But she started crying a bit later, before midnight my watch said, and Adam said it was too early to give her another bottle or we'd run out of milk. We didn't know what to do. I sang to her but it didn't make any difference and Adam laughed, but he soon stopped laughing and picked her up and walked round with her. She cried for a while and then she stopped but started again when he put her down, so he walked round some more and I went back to sleep. Then I woke up a bit later because she was crying again. Adam had been asleep but he got up and I had to get up too to scrub out the bottle again, and Adam fed her. The next time she woke up it was nearly four and Adam was asleep, and he wouldn't wake up except to say I was a girl and anyway it was my turn, so I picked her up and walked about with her. She sort of ended up with her face in my neck. It was very cold, even though the heater had been on all night, so I wrapped the fleece round both of us. It was hard to move about because there was so much stuff on the floor, and Adam as well, so I stood still and sort of rocked back and forth. I was near the window and I reached out and moved the blind back.

The light was grey outside, but the kind of grey you could tell would soon be morning rather than a wintry grey – there was a gleam in it. And you could see where there must have still been a bit of a breeze because the leaves on the hedge ruffled every now and again. All up one of the walls of the garden there's a rose bush and in summer roses grow in and out of the other plants. I hadn't noticed any yet this year, but it was strange, they must have been coming for a while because all in the shadows there were lighter patches and even in some places glints of white, and I knew they must be roses. I could see the dew on the long grass that grew against the shed step too.

The baby had gone to sleep. I didn't even really want to put her down anymore because I wasn't feeling tired. Well, in a way I felt very tired, but it was more that I felt peaceful and still, like I used to when I was little if Mum and Dad took us to a grown-up sort of party and we didn't get in the car to go home till late, or coming back from the beach after a hot day in the summer holidays. But I had a pain between my shoulders from holding her so I put her down. With not being sleepy the floor looked quite uncomfortable. My watch said it was twenty past four. You can't rely on Cal to stay asleep much past five most mornings, so I thought since I was awake I might as well go and have a look in the loft and see if I could find any baby clothes. Even if we told Mum today, the baby would still need clothes.

It was only when I got to the paved bit outside the back door and started tiptoeing that I thought about what I was going to do. It was one thing getting out Adam's window in the evening when I knew Mum was downstairs with music on. Even if I managed to get up the tree now without getting stuck, I had to get the window open wide enough to climb in – I was looking up at it and Adam had nearly closed it behind him – and then get in without waking Mum, and though it had felt like quite a cold night in the shed, she might easily have left her window open. If she heard someone coming in the window she'd think it was a burglar. Her room faced the front of the house, but Feng's window was the same side as Adam's and Cal's was just round the corner.

There wasn't anything else I could do, though. I could just go back to the shed for now and wait for Mum to unlock the back door, but the chances of us being able to sneak in without anyone seeing were rubbish. Now was the best time. She often said the reason she hated Cal waking so early was because he got her right out of the deepest sleep she had all night. So I started to climb up the tree.

It wasn't too scary actually. The worst thing was that it was really wet, and the wet was really cold. I was soaking by the time I got on top of the branch which scraped Adam's window. It was scary, leaning over to open it wide enough, because I had to use both hands and really pull, and as well as being afraid of falling I was afraid it would creak. But it didn't. I did knock a book off the desk, which was right by the window sill, and then the window scraped going back down, but no one woke up.

Our loft is just a junk room really, I suppose like most people's, though someone must have used it for something else once because it has a window and a little spiral staircase up to it instead of one of those metal ladders. There's an overhead light too, but it turned out that wasn't working so I had to pick my way across through all the boxes and chairs and open up the blind. Light flooded in. I'd never thought about it before but that room must have faced east because everything in it went gold, and when I shaded my eyes and looked out the window the roofs opposite were all black against the gold sky. I didn't want to go falling over things and making noise so I just stood looking round, and almost straight away I saw a pile of blankets which I thought might be useful in the shed.

When I moved the top blankets, which were quite thick and scratchy but would be softer than planks to lie on, I saw littler ones underneath, and in the middle of the pile

53

two of those baby blankets, the ones with the little holes in. One was white and one was blue. I thought that was terrific so I moved everything to get to them, and then underneath all that I found a baby basket. It had a tiny thin mattress in it, and two little raggy things I didn't recognise at first, but when I held them up I realised they must be sheets for it. I put the two blankets inside it and balanced it on top of a box of books, and looked around because I thought the baby clothes might be near the baby basket.

Actually the clothes were just in a bag in the middle of the room, a white bin liner one, and when I picked it up it tore and things came tumbling out. There wasn't much that looked like it might be the right size, just a little dress and matching cardigan I recognised, and a pair of dungarees and a couple of jumpers. One was knitted and one was a sweater with a hedgehog on it. Adam was born in winter so I thought they were probably his. The dress was the one I was wearing in the photograph of the day Mum and I came home from hospital. It was blue with white butterflies on it.

There weren't any vests or anything like that, but I thought the dress and jumpers and dungarees might be useful so I put them in the basket too. I thought I'd probably been in there a while, so before I went out I put the basket in the middle of one of the big blankets, another fleecy one, and wrapped it up, just in case. Then, on my way to the door, when I was reaching round to turn off the light, I saw a kettle sticking out of the top of a box of kitchen stuff. That felt really lucky.

As I got to the bottom of the steps I heard noises in Cal's room. With the kettle balanced on top of the huge pile of baby stuff I could barely see, so there was no way I could have got back upstairs without having a disaster. I galloped past Cal's door to my room and flung everything in just as Mum came out of his room. Her face was all puffy and tired. I think she must have not had her eyes open properly, because I'm not sure how she didn't see that I was bright red.

'Hello, lovey,' she said. 'What are you doing?'

'I just woke up,' I said. I do wake up early sometimes, though not very often. 'I couldn't go back to sleep. I was quiet, I don't think it was me that woke Cal.'

She made a *pffff* noise. 'He doesn't need an excuse. What have you got there?' The stupid flex of the kettle was trailing out from behind the door. I tried to kick it in and just made the door open more so that one of the blankets showed as well.

'A blanket and a kettle. Can we have them for the shed?' Adam wouldn't have said that, he would have thought of something else.

'God, I'd forgotten about that kettle. I don't suppose it works, but if it does, you can. What do you want the blanket for?'

'To put over the chair, like a throw.'

'All right, I suppose so. I should bung it in the wash first, it hasn't been used in a while from the colour of it. Are you going back to bed?'

'I might go downstairs and lie on the sofa. Are you?'

'Definitely. I've told Cal to go back to sleep but he might land on top of you soon.'

'OK. Shall I put a wash on then?'

She laughed. 'You're keen. You certainly could do. Do you know how to use the machine?'

I didn't, actually, but I said I did because it seemed like a really good chance to wash the things I'd found. I struggled into my room and hid the baby basket under my bed for later, and then took all the clothes and blankets and sheets down and put them in the washing machine. Then I bundled a lot of the other stuff from the wash bin in, though it didn't all fit and I had to put some back. I got the detergent and poured a lot of it into the drawer. I've watched Mum do that. Then I had a look at the dial. I wouldn't have known what temperature to wash the things on, but one of them said 'baby clothes', so I switched it on to that. I was afraid to leave the machine then, in case Mum came down after all and saw where the dial was, so I scrubbed out the bottle, which I'd brought back with me. When it was clean I suddenly thought that the baby might be screaming for it and Adam wouldn't be able to come and get it, so I unlocked the back door and ran out with it up the garden, round the corner and to the shed. The grass was still soaking and my legs were bare and got wet up to the knees. It was cold, but all the leaves on the bushes and hedges were edged with gold, and I kept seeing white roses everywhere. I couldn't think how I'd missed them before.

Adam shot up as if a truck had come through the wall when I ran in. He was half asleep so I just handed him the bottle and said I'd seen Mum so in a bit, once she was up, I'd try to nip back out so he could come in and show himself. I told him about the basket and the clothes too. We could bring those out once Mum and Feng and Cal had gone swimming. Then I went back inside.

I was just drying my legs with a tea towel when Cal clomped down the stairs and put the TV on full blast for Sunday-morning cartoons.

'It's a bit loud,' I said to him.

'So what?'

I sat down gingerly next to him on the sofa, since I had nothing else to do. It was strange being up so early, especially on a Sunday. 'Is this one any good?'

'No.'

'Why are you watching it, then?'

He sighed loudly and stretched his foot out suddenly so that it bashed my leg. 'I'm not allowed to stay upstairs

after six and I'm not allowed on the Wii before breakfast.'
Weekends used to be the exception to that because there
was no rush in the mornings, but of course Dad used to
get up early so he was there to keep an eye on Cal.

'I could read you a story,' I offered doubtfully.

'No,' he said, and kicked me again.

'Well, I could put the Wii on for you now if you want.
Mum won't mind, since I'm up, and it's the weekend.'

He sat up. 'Will you play it with me?'

'I can't, I've got all this stuff to do.'

'Are you coming swimming?'

'Not today.' I set up the Wii for him and then went back
into the kitchen.

Chapter Five

It was such a busy morning, even though I'd been up so early. By nine o'clock, which is when Stephen the social worker came round, I felt as if I'd lived a whole day without even having any breakfast. I was starving too. I'd had to just mill around for a while, since there wasn't any point me swapping with Adam till Mum was there to see him, and anyway I had to make sure Cal didn't do anything terrible to the Wii. Part of the reason he was extra hard work just then was because he'd broken his last DS in a temper and the new one, his third one, hadn't come yet. When he broke the first Dad said if he did it again he'd never get a new one, but they had to give in because it's one of the things that make him bearable. Mum said she didn't know how kids like Cal existed before we had all this technology, or how their families existed, and Dad said had it ever occurred to her that maybe they didn't because maybe computers and our lifestyle these days are actually to blame for Cals in the first place, but Mum just scoffed and said what an arbitrary thing to say in the light of what we knew Cal had been through, and you might as well blame his red hair for his temper and the way he was. Then Dad got angry and said she was being completely fatuous and he hoped she would never say something like that in front of Cal. They'd been using words like arbitrary and fatuous a lot lately.

So after he'd attacked me a few times he woke Feng up, and Mum got up and started running up and down the stairs getting Feng dressed and getting breakfast for them so that they'd be ready for Stephen, and that was when I noticed that it wasn't just the washing machine dial I had to worry about – you could see the little dress and the jumper, and the dungarees, and the blue and white blankets, whirling round and round. The machine was going plinkerty-tonk, plinkerty-tonk, like it was begging Mum to look at it, and when it started spinning I thought it was going to take off, but she didn't even glance at it. And then it came to rest and finished. At least I could spin the dial then when no one was looking, but that butterfly dress was right at the front. I stood hiding it, pretending to sweep all the toast crumbs onto a plate till Mum went rushing upstairs again to get dressed herself, and then I threw everything out of the machine and into the tumble dryer, which hasn't got a window, and switched it on.

Then I had to fly upstairs, and Mum met me in the hall so I had to go into my room and spend a few minutes there, and it was so hard not to just climb into bed and pull the duvet over my head. Then I crept into Adam's room and climbed down the tree as fast as I could so I could send in Adam, who was really impatient and said he'd been waiting for hours and he was starving. I sat with the baby, who'd just had the absolute last of the milk, and started singing to her to keep her from wailing just as the social worker was coming. I'd remembered some other songs, some that Mum sang, but they were all so sad, about troubles and suffering and grief and people doing terrible things to each other, and I thought that might be all right for some babies but this one had enough problems of her own, so I sang 'Humpty-Dumpty' to her, and 'Jack and Jill', but then I thought that they weren't exactly happy songs so I stuck with 'Twinkle Twinkle Little Star' and 'I Had a Little Nut-Tree' and 'Old King Cole'. It was hard to sound cheerful when I kept thinking about Leanne and wondering where she was now. Some of the time the baby looked quite a lot like her, even though most of the time she just looked like any baby. She had sticky eyes. I thought I'd better see on the Internet what to do about them or she might be going blind or something for all we knew.

She didn't go to sleep but just lay there looking at me, whether I held her or laid her on the ground. I was lying down beside her on the blanket and had almost gone off to sleep again when I nearly had a fit because there was this tremendous scraping noise against the wall of the shed and then a big thump right above where we were lying, but it was only Adam. He'd told Mum he was going out, because he was meant to be meeting his friends, then nipped round the alley at the back of the house and climbed over the garden wall. It's a high wall and he'd slid down on our side and kicked the shed by accident. He looked exhausted.

'You look terrible,' I said.

'*I* look terrible! At least I've changed my clothes.' It was true, I'd completely forgotten to take off yesterday's clothes. Normally Mum would have noticed. Now I wondered whether I should just keep these ones on; she might notice the difference otherwise.

'Wait while I call Dan and tell him I'm not coming,' he said, getting out his phone. 'Don't want him ringing the house looking for me.'

'What shall I do if she cries while you're talking,' I asked. 'Hang a blanket over her?'

'I'll just tell him it's a foster kid if I have to.'

'What were you supposed to be doing?'

'I don't know,' he said impatiently, 'the usual,

I suppose. Playing computer games and talking about boobs.'

He had a stupid conversation and put Dan off. He sounded different, talking to his friends – much more friendly, compared to how he looked on the end of the phone, rolling his eyes and pulling faces. He gets tired of people easily. But he thought it was important to have a social life and spend time outside of home and school with people his age. He was always hounding me about my friends too, and about getting some that I actually wanted to spend time with. But you can't just pick out who you want to be your friends, at least I couldn't. And the ones I had were all right. My best friend, Amy, had gone off to boarding school of all things so I didn't see her very much, but I still had a couple of my primary-school friends in my year. So it was OK, it was just that I didn't much enjoy the stuff we did or the things we talked about, mainly because we'd been doing it all so long. I don't know if it would have been different if Amy was still around, maybe not. It was like we were all waiting to move on to the next thing, and afraid that we never would.

I went back to the house. Already I didn't have to think so much about climbing up and down that tree. The hardest part now was nipping past the kitchen window in case anyone inside might be looking out. The doorbell rang just as I was going downstairs and I heard Cal letting Stephen in, which I knew Mum wouldn't like because Cal isn't meant to open the front door. If he does he sometimes just keeps going. Mum was trying to stuff enough towels into the big hemp bag. She left them spilling out on the hall floor and sat Stephen down on the sofa while she took Feng to the toilet.

I stayed downstairs with Cal so that he wouldn't do anything to Stephen before Mum was finished with Feng. Stephen was lying back on the sofa with his legs crossed. He tried to talk to Cal but Cal was just jumping around, so he looked at me and said, 'And how are you, Phoebe?' I said I was fine. He said, 'It must be tough for you guys, though, with your dad staying somewhere else? How are you handling it?' I wanted to say that it was absolutely none of his business how I felt about my dad moving out, but I couldn't. Anyway, in a way it *was* his business. I just felt like it shouldn't have been. So I said I was fine, really, and went to pick up the towels and put them in the bag.

Normally I would have helped Mum get the kids in the car, but she had Stephen, and I was dying to get back out to the shed, so I went upstairs and got the basket and the kettle from where they were hidden, and our moneyboxes and another clean towel, since it seemed like towels would always come in useful, and then crept down the stairs and waited by the window till I saw them drive off.

Adam was delighted when I arrived with the kettle, and said now we'd have loads of money for everything else, and even more delighted with the basket. He said no one would be able to tell the difference now between our baby and anyone else's, or at least they wouldn't after I'd been shopping. It took us a while to make the shopping list, and even once we'd finished Adam said I'd better take the pen in case I kept thinking of things on the bus to the supermarket. It was a very long list.

'Am I really doing this?' I asked. 'I mean, this is going to cost a lot of money. And we haven't really decided that it's for the best, have we? I mean, we're both pretty knackered already. If we're just going to tell Mum later on today or something, there's no point in doing all this shopping now.'

'She'll still need it all, whoever's in charge of her,' Adam said tersely.

'Yes, but...' I scuffed my toe against the floor. 'It wouldn't be us paying for it, though.'

'Oh, for God's sake, Phoebe. I'm sure Mum will refund you, if that's what you're worried about.' He had a disgusted expression on his face. He was right in a way anyway, I didn't care too much; I don't get all that much pocket money but it mounts up quite quickly since Mum still pays for my clothes and everything, and whenever I'm doing anything that costs a bit she tends to give me the money, like when I go to the cinema and places like that. I'd been thinking about an iPod, but then my birthday was coming up soon. The thing was, though, I felt like this was a jumping-off point, even more than when Adam hadn't come in to dinner the night before.

'Adam,' I said, 'tell me why we're doing this. Why you want to do it.'

'I don't want her to go into Care.'

'But,' I persisted, 'this is only going to keep her out of Care for a couple of days, or something. Because I can't see how we're going to make it work. Even if we get all this stuff and learn how to look after her, we can't just constantly be in the shed, for one thing, not even one at a time. Mum will notice.'

'I just want to give it a try.'

'Why? What's the point, if we can't do it for long?'

'Look, Phoebe, it's the right thing to do.'

'Mum's going to go nuts when she does find out.'

'She's already nuts. She's got too much to cope with with Feng and especially Cal already.'

'Well, exactly.'

'Yeah.' He was much more ruffled than he usually gets. 'So, do you think it's going to make her feel better to have to take Leanne's baby, that she left here specially, and ditch her into Care? Knowing she'll turn into another Cal, or another Leanne for that matter? Mum and Dad are in a mess right now and they're screwing things up for all of us, especially Feng and Cal, but at least Mum's still holding on to them, and I can't do anything about all that. I can about this. It's the right thing to do to keep her and I'm not having her thrown overboard just because Mum and Dad can't sort their stuff out right now.'

He bent over the baby, who had both feet stuck up in the air so that the blanket was all rucked up over her middle. I watched them. 'How are we going to manage with school, and everything?'

'We'll take some time off. That should make you happy.'

'Well, what about all your stuff? You're always doing your swimming, or visiting your old people and whatever.' Adam is all into keeping busy and doing impressive things.

'I'll bin all that for a while.'

'What, really? Even your swimming?'

'Yes. I'm prepared to do that. OK?'

I was quiet for a bit. 'What makes you think we can do it, if Mum or Dad couldn't, or Leanne, either?'

'Because we're going to put our minds to it, which is more than anyone else would do.'

He'd got to me again, and I stopped arguing and picked up the list. Adam said to be careful which checkout I went to and to avoid any nosy old ladies, though I had a plan if anyone asked to say my dad was picking my mum up from hospital today and the baby had come a bit early so we didn't have everything we needed. Adam said not to look nervous, and not to be too long because she was going to go off once she got hungry because there was no more milk, and for goodness' sake to keep an eye out for anyone we knew. I said if he had the chance he could wash the clothes we'd taken off her last night, and do the rest of the stuff in the laundry bin while he was at it.

It's a bus ride and then quite a long walk to the really big supermarket. We'd done it before because we've only got one car so if it breaks down or Mum ever goes away in it or anything, that's how we get there.

There were two whole aisles all to do with baby stuff. I didn't want to look suspicious so I tried to believe the story I'd made up about why someone like me would be doing baby shopping, and just walked up and down as many times as I needed to. It was hard to see everything, there was so much. I left the nappies till the end because they were so heavy and took up the whole trolley. I got loads of cotton wool and some of those cotton bud things even though I couldn't see what you'd use them for, but the box said they were for babies and they were only cheap, and bin liners to put the nappies and everything else in, and a packet of muslin cloths, which turned out to be just like the things Mum used to clean her face, because all the websites said you should have them. Then I got a bottle of special baby bubble bath because we were going to try to give her a bath, and I was just looking at the baby bathtubs and thinking I was never going to get all the way home with one of those when I remembered that I'd read last night that some babies prefer an upright bath that's shaped more like a bucket because they feel safer and you can have the water deeper. So I nipped up a couple of aisles to the 'household' stuff and got a grey bucket. It had a bit at the top where you could squeeze a mop, but that came off. It only cost three pounds, which was about the same as the bottle of bubble bath.

Then I went to get milk. The cartons were super expensive, and I was just thinking that there was no way we were going to be able to afford her when I saw that there were big tubs next to them. I read the side and figured out that now we had a kettle, dried milk was easily the cheapest and wouldn't need keeping in a fridge, either. So I got a tub of that, and a box of four bottles, and some sterilising tablets. For clothes I got the things that were on special offer – second pack half-price – so two packs of vests and two of sleepsuits, and then a romper suit that had short legs and arms in case it got hot, and three pairs of socks to go with the dress and the dungarees at home as well, and five bibs, and a sunhat with a strap under the chin. And then I bought her a small soft panda because I thought she should have something to hold, and Leanne hadn't left anything. There were a few soft books which I looked at for a while because I'd read that you should read to babies and get them used to books straight away, which I agreed with, but they weren't very nice and I wasn't sure I'd added up the costs of everything right, so I thought I'd remember to have a look in the loft and see if there were any there instead, or even go to the library if we could think of any excuse to borrow baby books.

It had all taken ages because of having to do the sums. I lurked in one of the aisles trying to decide which checkout to go to. It was hard because I had to watch out for the other people standing in line as well as the people working there. In the end I got served by a teenage boy who spent the whole time looking over my head, so that was all right. I spent more than eighty pounds, which was way more than I could ever remember spending on my own. It left us with practically nothing.

The bucket was quite useful really, having a handle; I could never have carried a bathtub as well as all the nappies and the milk tub and all the lighter things. It was hard enough anyway getting to the bus stop.

Then an old lady started talking to me on the bus about my baby sister – I told her my story and she seemed pleased and got very friendly. 'Arh, it'll be nice to have your mum home as well, won't it? And what's the baby called?'

I hadn't thought of an answer to that, we didn't know the baby's name. 'Summer,' I said, because it was, and then felt silly because I don't even like the name Summer and I don't think I look anywhere near girly and fairyish enough to have a little sister called that. Then she started looking in my bucket and bags at everything I'd bought and I got nervous and got off the bus two stops early. I'd had a rest so I could manage all right but I was anxious about bumping into anyone I knew.

I was even more anxious when I got to our front door because I could hear the baby crying. It was a very still day, being Sunday and sunny, and there was no wind. No one lived very near us, and it wasn't exactly hot so perhaps no one would have their windows open, but still I thought it was a bit worrying because it meant Mum would have been able to hear her if she was there. I dashed through the house and out to the shed, and she really was yelling, I'd never heard a baby cry so loud. Adam was bright red with carrying her and shushing her. He started yelling at me for taking so long, and I was wishing I'd thought to buy at least one carton so we wouldn't have to boil a kettle and wait for the milk to cool down, but the thing that really took

71

a while was sterilising the bottles. I filled up the bucket at the tap and threw in three tablets because I didn't have time to try to figure out how many litres there are in a bucket, and unscrewed all the bottles and dropped them all over the place and threw them in the bucket and splashed Adam, who was leaning over me . . . it was like some TV sitcom.

We used the fifteen minutes, while we waited for the bottles to sterilise, to boil the kettle and break all the clothes out and get a little pile of muslins and open a pack of nappies. Adam fetched the clothes and blankets and sheets from the dryer, and we made up the basket, all while she was howling so much that we got more or less used to it, though my heart was beating very, very fast.

I found myself talking nonsense to her, saying everything I was doing out loud in a soothing voice, not that it soothed her at all. When the time was up, we put the bottles back together and poured the water out on the grass, and Adam kneeled down and got ready to undress the baby for a bath while I made a bottle up. It was hard. We decided to make too much, because she hadn't really had enough in the night, and there was so much in that tub we couldn't imagine using it all any time soon, so I made up half a bottle and only spilled a bit of the milk powder on the floor, and put it in the jug from the bathroom that was full of cold water so it would cool down.

The kettle had boiled again by then so we made up the bath. That was hard too because we didn't want to add too much cold so we kept flapping it with different fingers to test the temperature, but we ran out of fingers in the end, and used our elbows, and it was only on the fourth elbow, my left one, that we decided it was cool enough. I thought she'd been crying as high as she could and as loud, but when Adam lowered her in, holding her under the arms, the bubbles went up round her face and she hit a new pitch. I felt like my heart was going to jump up into my head. Making sure her neck was clean was the hardest part because there was so much skin there and she couldn't have held her head up even if she'd understood I wanted her to. We sloshed water all over her and broke open the cotton buds to clean the corners of her eyes.

Adam was about ready to drop her by this point so I laid the towel out and he sort of muffled her into it so we could dry her properly. We rubbed her hair gently too, and put a nappy on her and a new vest and one of the sleepsuits, and she was lovely. She'd stopped crying in the towel, and just lay looking at us, and her chin kept shaking even though she wasn't sad anymore. Adam wrapped her in the blue blanket I'd found in the loft, which was much softer than the one she'd had, and sat down, and I brought him the bottle and we managed to get a bib round her neck.

I sat down too then and watched. It was so nice that she was clean and in clothes that we'd bought just for her, and especially that she'd stopped crying, I felt almost happy. We were doing all right so far; she was in better shape than she had been when her mother was looking after her, and I was almost glad that we hadn't told anyone. But I couldn't stay there for long. The swimming pool isn't that far away, and I knew Mum would be back soon to feed Feng and Cal lunch, and anyway I hadn't had anything to eat all day so I went back in. Adam said I could take a turn in the afternoon because he was going to the library to see if he could get a book about babies and what they were supposed to be doing at her age. He said he wasn't going to have our baby grow up stupid.

Chapter Six

Even though I'd only been back in the house ten minutes, just enough time to pull last night's baby clothes out of the washing machine and hide them in my room and sit down on the sofa, I was asleep when the front door opened. It was lucky Stephen didn't come in or he might have thought I needed taking into Care, Mum said. She asked why I was still wearing yesterday's clothes and I said I'd got up too early and I'd go and change. We had sandwiches for lunch, and then Mum said Feng and Cal had to have a rest. She'd picked up a DVD for them on the way home so Cal didn't kick off about it. I said I might do some revision as I had exams coming the week after, and I thought I might do it in the shed, now that we had a kettle there. I made a kind of a joke out of it and Mum didn't seem to think it was that weird. She looked as if she wished she had a shed to escape to too.

When I got out there with a couple of my books the baby was asleep and Adam was restless. It was Sunday so the library would be shut, but he said he was going to go into town to the bookshop and scope out books that might be useful, so he headed off over the fence.

Actually I did get some revision done. I don't find it very easy learning things, especially when it's a load of different things at once, and normally when I have tests coming up Mum or Dad or Adam help me, but no one had had much time lately. Mum had said we'd squeeze some in this week, even if it meant Dad having to come round and actually spend some time with us. I don't mind revision too much when someone is helping, even Adam can be quite fun when he's trying to think of ways to help you remember things, but now I started hoping no one would remember, because everyone had enough going on already, and exams didn't really seem that important.

But the baby slept for quite a while, and when I got tired of looking at my history book I lay down next to her on a sleeping bag and tried to remember what I'd just been learning. I fell asleep again, and then Adam was back.

He'd found lots of titles for us to look for in the library when it was open, and had a good flick through some of them till he got kicked out of that department by a suspicious shop attendant. He had a great long list of picture books to try and borrow too; he said they'd been delighted with him on the children's floor when he'd told them he was looking for books for his baby sister.

Perhaps we shouldn't have bothered saying that Adam was out at a friend's house, because now we didn't have a way to feed him properly. We hadn't had enough money left for him to buy anything while he was out and he made a huge fuss about missing lunch. On the other hand it meant I could just go in and out and leave the baby with him.

He said I should get a good night's sleep because I was on duty the next day. He said I had to be the one to bunk off school for the next couple of days because he'd just finished his exams and he absolutely had to be in school to get his results and go through his papers in class or his teachers would get in a tizzy and start phoning Mum. Of course, he wouldn't believe that any of the teachers at my school would notice if I went missing for two years or got squashed by a lorry outside the front door, and besides, this was the last week before my exams so we wouldn't be studying anything new. And because his school is private he breaks up for the holidays ages before me, so he could take his turn then.

I got the collywobbles again when he was talking about holidays, because even his didn't start for another three weeks, and it had been hard enough looking after the baby and not getting caught for one day, not to mention expensive. But we'd had that conversation already and anyway by then he was all cock-a-hoop with us for getting this far. I did have a problem, though.

'It's the meeting about the play tomorrow, after school,' I told him.

'So?'

'I'm not missing it. I won't get a part.'

He sighed. 'Is it really that important, getting some part with no lines in another crappy school play?'

I could have got offended but I knew that wasn't really what he thought. Normally he's all about me being in plays, because it's the only thing I do really, though he'd prefer it if I got leading roles; last year he nagged me for weeks beforehand to put myself up for a bigger part. 'Yes. I'm not missing it.' I love the school play. They do a big one every summer, and loads of people come to see it; we used to go even when I was at primary school, and I looked forward to it for years before I started secondary. Really there was no chance of me getting a decent part, since you have to be pretty special or the drama teacher's niece or something to get many lines when you're my age, but I just like being in them. They're quite intense because they don't even start the rehearsals till after exam week. It's something different, you get to meet different people, or see them differently, and I like the performances too.

He shook his head. 'I'm giving up all my things. You obviously don't have the same level of commitment.'

'No, I don't. Anyway, you're talking about missing a couple of swimming sessions. If I miss this I miss the whole play, and there won't be another one till next year.'

'All right,' he said, sighing even more deeply. 'What time's the meeting?'

'Four o'clock.'

'Fine. I'll skip games and come home early and you can go in for it. But if any of your teachers see you, try and look sick, OK? You'll have to be ready to explain why you weren't there for lessons, and won't be the day after, either.'

Sunday evenings are always a mix of peacefulness and miserableness, I suppose like they are for everyone. That evening, just after I'd come back from the shed and was slipping out of Adam's room, Mum started shouting in the big bathroom and cursing everything. It was because she couldn't find the jug to rinse Cal's hair. I'd left it in the shed. Of course we needed one in the shed, but I should have remembered to get another one from the supermarket where they were cheap, and brought Mum's back in. She was shouting for all of us to search our rooms for it, so I had to pretend to go and ask Adam to look too while Mum was on her knees holding soapy Cal in place in the bath and trying to dig around in the cupboard behind it as well. I was scared she'd come running into the room herself, but what I really felt bad about was making things so hard for her when she'd had a rotten day, anyway. Every day was rotten for her at the moment. I brought her a saucepan in the end.

I said it to Adam the next morning, how rough things were on Mum and that it was a shame we had to keep hiding away in the shed and not helping out. I'd felt bad leaving her to read to Feng again too, especially when I'd already not done reading practice with him in the afternoon – and about not at least chatting to her in the evening once the boys were in bed. She'd looked really sad when I left her downstairs to go to bed, but I was so tired. Adam said again what did I think she'd prefer to worry about – a missing plastic jug or ditching a brand-new baby, not to mention Leanne?

I really hadn't wanted to go to the shed that morning. It was all complicated, trying to coordinate things so the baby wasn't left alone and Adam and I both had the chance to get dressed and eat breakfast and leave, and even though I'd slept all night I was so tired. When I went out the front door all I wanted to do was walk up the road to school, dead slowly. I usually cut through the park on the way and it was a nice morning. But I knew Adam would be waiting so I went round the corner, and he was already on the alleyway side, ready to hiss at me for taking so long and bunt me up the wall.

It took me ages to be ready to jump off the other side. I'd never liked climbing down from walls, I always scraped my back. But Adam was there grumbling, and I knew if Mum went up to her room and happened to look out of her window in the right direction she might see me teetering on the top, so I slid down it in the end and only scratched my leg on a thorn. I sort of wished Mum had more time to spend hanging around in her bedroom in the mornings so that she could have caught sight of me. I felt bad for thinking it though.

It's amazing how long a day can seem when all you're doing is hanging around waiting for someone to go to sleep, and then worrying that they're going to wake up, but it was all right. I managed not to think about what would happen if I got caught skiving, because after all if we were caught that would probably be the least of my problems. In a way I didn't mind missing school, I never liked it that much, and because she did sleep a lot I sort of got some revision done, though I was too dozy most of the time. Also, with everyone out, I could just drop everything and pick her up as soon as she started working herself up, so she hardly cried at all. But it was boring and I was relieved when Adam finally dropped over the wall, especially because he was late.

'I got caught,' he said very grumpily. He was wearing his sports kit. 'Bloody cricket. I had to sneak off in the middle, I'm going to be in trouble tomorrow.'

'See you,' I said, snatching my bag up.

'It better be worth it,' he called after me. 'You better get the main part.'

I did creep into school, because Adam was right, it would be hard to explain to my form teacher how I was in the middle of a terrible illness but was well enough to be there for the play meeting. If I'd been one of the school stars I could have skipped it, of course, and just told Mr Rossy later that week I wanted to be in the play. Shantel Hardwick swanned in fifteen minutes late but that didn't matter, we all knew she'd get whatever part she wanted.

'Look at her,' my friend Charlotte, who always does the plays too, whispered. I did look at her – she wasn't even wearing school uniform, except that she had all her amazing blonde ringlets screwed up in one of the terrible maroon scrunchies that not even I would have worn, not even when I was in the first year. As if that counted as uniform and it didn't matter that the rest of what she was wearing was a lemon-coloured T-shirt over a red and green checked skirt. Shantel Hardwick is strange, sort of like a famous person. In last year's play I'd been one of her children, so I'd watched her a lot, and I wasn't even sure she was that good an actress. It was just that she had this sort of beam about her that made everyone look at her.

There wasn't really any need for her to wear the kind of clothes she did, they would have looked anyway, whether she was onstage or off it.

'She looks ridiculous,' my friend Marika said, as if that was the last word, folding her arms over her chest like her mother does.

'Oh, it's not that bad,' I said. 'Better than uniform, anyway.' Actually most of the time I'm delighted we have a uniform because I can't imagine having to choose what to wear every single morning, not to mention buying it in the first place, but you tend not to say things like that out loud.

It was going to be a musical that summer, which was sort of a shame because I can't sing at all, or dance. But Mr Rossy lived with one of the music teachers, Miss Bude, and they usually did a musical every other summer, so we'd known it was coming. Marika wouldn't have come otherwise; she's got no time for plays, but she thinks she's going to be a great singer.

We found out it was going to be something called *Return to the Forbidden Planet*, which sounded like a sequel but apparently wasn't. No one seemed to have heard of it, but we all got scripts straight away and the auditions were right then, though rehearsals wouldn't start till after exams. Mr Rossy split us up into groups, according to whether we wanted big parts, middle parts or small parts. He said that if you auditioned for a big part and didn't get one it doesn't mean he wouldn't give you a smaller one, but of course it takes a lot of face to say you're going for a big part. Hardly anyone does. I would definitely have been too embarrassed, so maybe that shows I'm not exactly meant to be a star.

Charlotte and Marika and I all went for the middle parts line for the first time. 'We won't get them,' I said.

'Oh well. So what?' Charlotte has to giggle to psych herself up but she's better at it than me.

'I'm going for it, anyway,' Marika announced, and left us behind. She'd got this very intense look on her face. She wanted a part with a solo number.

'Come on, then,' I said, and walked up to the line just behind Charlotte. She stopped and tried to get behind me but I shoved her ahead and we both got the giggles, which I could see Marika thought was all very unprofessional from where she was standing, between two fifth years. I get very nervous in these situations, but I was relieved that at least I wouldn't have to listen to Adam telling me off for days about being a scaredy cat and selling myself short only going for the smallest parts.

Then, when I got to the front, Mr Rossy was just coming over from the other section of the hall. 'Er, what's your name again?' he shouted at me, as if I was deaf. 'Right, Phoebe. Can you sing, Phoebe?'

'Er...' I said.

He made me *sing*. I couldn't believe it. I should probably have just said no, but Mr Rossy is one of those hypnotic people. He told me to sing whatever I liked, then when I couldn't think of anything he tapped his foot and told me to sing something from a musical. All that would come into my head was *Annie*, so I swallowed about seven times and started singing 'Hard-Knock Life.' I was very bad, but it wouldn't have been as humiliating if Shantel Hardwick hadn't started doing a Jay-Z impression in the background. I wished I hadn't stuck up for her and her outfit.

After about a minute, I suppose, which felt like eighteen years, Mr Rossy told me I could stop, looking disappointed. He didn't even stay for me to read out my lines, but left me with Mrs Clarkson who's like his dogsbody, and started wandering around again. I wiped my sweaty face on my shirt and thought it was probably some kind of message that I should have stayed safely in the shed, where you didn't get humiliated in front of hundreds of people.

'It was all right,' Charlotte said kindly, when she'd found me lurking near the doorway where no one was sitting. 'It would have been much better if you'd known the words.'

'I know.'

'You should have picked one you knew, really. Anyway, you were better than me.'

'I was not,' I said. Actually, I hadn't heard a single word of her audition, because my ears hadn't stopped ringing yet. I could barely hear Marika, who was singing again just then, though she was giving it loads as she always does.

'Look at her now,' Charlotte said scornfully, nodding at Shantel Hardwick who was doing some kind of loose-legged high-kneed dance steps up on the actual stage, with all the teachers watching her raptly. 'I don't know why they don't just put her in a sparkly bikini and let the audience look at her for an hour and a half, instead of doing a play; it's what they really want to do.'

I laughed, but really it was closer to the truth than I wanted to hear, I think, and I felt sorry for myself. Actually, I felt sorry for most of us there. I mean, there wasn't much chance of any of the three of us, for instance, getting a biggish part. Marika is short and skinny and very dark with a thick fringe that falls below her eyes, and my mum says she looks like a small Mexican child in an old cowboy film. Charlotte is a lot more chunky and brassy with long braids, and then there's me. I wasn't keen on hanging around anymore; I wanted to get home to where it was safe. And when I did, I didn't even have to talk too much about the audition. Adam was too busy reading books to the baby.

***

For the whole of that first week we got into the habit of spending the evenings – after school and before dinner, and sometimes after dinner too – in the shed together; we said Adam was helping me revise. That was the nicest time of the day because it was so much easier looking after her with two, and less lonely. Most of the time we weren't talking or anything, just sort of grunting when the baby needed something doing, but it was more time than we'd spent in the same room, just the two of us, for years and years.

The nights were the hardest time because you were more tired, and it felt so strange being up on your own in the dark with no one in the next room – no next room at all. I got scared the first couple of nights on my own in there, but that was a stupid reason to want to stop doing it, and I did get used to all the noises. There were even owls, and foxes screaming sometimes, but I got so that I just got cross with them for waking the baby. Adam kept bringing my school books out, one by one, in the evenings, as if he really thought this was the perfect chance for me to finally start working hard and become a genius like him, but I managed to sneak some proper books out too, so at least when she wouldn't go to sleep and I had to be walking round, I could read *What Katy Did* or *A Little Princess*, or some other book I'd read a million times before. Comfort reading, Mum calls it.

For company I started talking to the baby. I suppose it was just like talking to myself, really, but I thought someone ought to speak to her and let her know things were all right. After all, Adam and I were all she had. Sometimes, if I said something after being quiet for a while, she would turn her head towards me.

There were still times when I'd be up at the house and it was my turn to go to the shed, and I really didn't want to. I got very attached to my bedroom and its nice blue walls and pools of warm yellow light in the evenings, and my bed that was long enough to stretch out on. It was just really hard not being able to go and watch TV or have a bath or just lie on the sofa and do nothing because the things to do were endless, even when the baby was asleep. Just the washing took an unbelievable amount of time. I suppose being so tired didn't help.

Even when I was so zonked that things seemed all out of proportion though, which was a lot of the time, there was something nice as well as hard about being so busy. Before the baby, for a long time I'd been thinking dreary thoughts about myself. I mean, things at home weren't the easiest, someone was always causing trouble, and then Mum and Dad had been arguing for what felt like years, but the days at school were all alike and just boring. Even at weekends all I did was go to the cinema with Marika and Charlotte, or round their houses sometimes. I hardly ever heard from Amy anymore, either, and sometimes I'd catch myself imagining what it must be like for her at boarding school, some kind of cross between Malory Towers and a big drug-fuelled no-parent carnival. Meanwhile there were people in my class who were already doing things outside school like getting drunk and going to parties and having boyfriends, the kind of stuff I couldn't see myself doing for years and years. I didn't really want any of that but I was bored of what I was doing; and now I had something different. I wasn't just being an average child all the time. And it was nice being the one to do something that needed doing. I could see what Adam meant.

One night when I was in the house, and I was trying to help Feng with his homework for a few minutes because Cal had gone mental again over the TV being turned off and Mum had had to take him upstairs, I noticed how glum Feng seemed. It was unusual. He used to get tearful and sad sometimes, but he was never gloomy.

'What's wrong?' I asked.

'Oh – Cal.' He gouged a hole in his paper with a pencil.

'Don't let him bother you.'

'It's not that. It's that he's so upset. I'm worried about him,' he explained.

'Well. That's . . . sweet.'

He looked at me with his shiny serious eyes. 'He's missing your dad.'

I felt for Feng but I didn't buy it all that much, to be honest. 'He sees him all the time, you both do, don't you? Practically as much as you ever did.' It was funny that Dad had been so reluctant over Feng and Cal in the first place, but now when he was in the house he spent far more time with them than with Adam or me.

'Yes, but it's not the same.'

'I know,' I said, trying to be consoling. 'Yeah, I know. It's adjusting. We all miss him.'

'No,' he said, shaking his head and picking up his pencil again. 'That's not what's the problem. Phoebe, if he never does come back, he'll still be your dad and Adam's, won't he?'

'Yeah.'

'He won't be ours,' he said simply.

Maybe I should have told Mum about it but I didn't want to make her feel worse than she already did. Anyway, I didn't get the chance. I got hardly any time just cuddling up with Mum and chatting at the moment. She was probably too busy, anyway. But even though I saw her every morning and every evening I felt as if we were miles and miles apart, and I was homesick.

I had thought we might squeeze some time in on the Thursday evening, because Dad was taking the boys out for tea, but I had to go out, even though it was a school night. Mum had said to me the day before, 'Catrina Coverly called me today. She said Amy's home for the week.'

'Why?' I asked.

'Study leave, before her exams, would you believe.' She raised her eyes to heaven. 'She's off to her dad's on Friday, so Catrina asked whether you'd like to go round after school tomorrow. Honestly, you'd think that woman didn't know anyone beside herself could have any prior arrangements. But I knew you'd like to see Amy so I said you could.'

Adam was cross when I told him, but I couldn't help it. It was only going to be for a few extra hours, anyway.

Thursday was the first day I'd been to school all week, but people were sort of worried about exams the next week, and sort of fed up because the sunny weather had gone, and no one really asked me what had been wrong with me. I'd been quite worried about skipping three days – I'd definitely pretended to be iller than I was, before now, to get days off, but Mum and Dad had always known where I was; I'd never bunked off before. It was odd to know that I could if I wanted to, and not even my friends would notice.

'Where were you?' Charlotte did ask me, when I was trying not to eat all my sandwiches at morning break.

'I had a bug,' I said.

'You looked all right on Monday at the auditions.'

'Yeah. It came back.' I'm sure she thought I'd been skipping because I was embarrassed about my audition. As if Mum would have let me.

I went straight from school to Amy's on the bus, and it did feel a bit strange being away from the baby for so long. Amy's house is quite a long way from ours and I hadn't even passed it in a long time, but I used to know it well. It was sort of really posh in a certain kind of way. It wasn't enormous or anything, but it was on a nice road of sweet little houses with nice front gardens full of flowers, and her mother had made a mosaic of fish and mermaids on the kitchen wall. It's the kind of thing that sets Mum off but I always liked it.

Catrina, Amy's mother, opened the door and hugged me. She was exactly the same, with very long red nails and smart short hair with gold tips and a very piercing voice. She was always nice to me, though it used to be a bit embarrassing whenever something went wrong, because she was the kind of mother who would tell Amy off in front of me. Then Amy came trooping down the stairs. I was quite surprised because she looked different. She'd grown out her fringe and got thinner, I thought, but also she was wearing different sorts of clothes. She had this thin black top on that was almost see-through.

Since she'd gone away it was so different from when we used to play every day in the week at school, and most weekends as well, that it was always a bit awkward at first, but usually only for a few minutes till we started talking about something. This time was worse. Her mum was fussing around trying to give me biscuits, even though Amy said she wouldn't eat them because she didn't eat biscuits anymore. Well, there wasn't any way I could eat them after that, even though they were gorgeous-looking honey chocolate thick ones and Catrina was desperate for me not to say no just because Amy had. She almost ordered Amy to eat one, so that was embarrassing.

Then, when she left us on our own, somehow it wasn't easy to talk, either. Amy told me about how she was sort of thinking about going out with someone at her school, but she didn't like him all that much, really. Also he didn't live anywhere nearby, he was from Yorkshire where he lived in, like, a mansion because his parents were both surgeons, or something. Then we talked about holidays – her dad was taking her to Ibiza in the summer, though not the clubby bit, obviously – and then she asked me if I'd been in any more plays. I told her about the audition, which made her laugh. Amy was into dancing, all kinds, a new one every time I saw her. We used to do ballet together years and years ago when we were really small, but I gave it up early because she was so much better than me, and she always wanted to concentrate hard during the class and not whisper or giggle.

So hearing about her dancing sort of made me glaze over, which wasn't very fair when she'd asked me about plays, but we wound up talking about Charlotte and Marika. We were all friends at primary school but me and Amy were always best friends. She didn't really see them anymore except sometimes with me, for my birthdays and things. They were an easy thing for us to talk about because we always seemed to end up giggling about them, things like how bossy Charlotte is and how Marika can't sing even though she thinks she's brilliant. But somehow I didn't like it this time.

Then she asked me about my family. She knew about Dad moving out but we didn't really go into it. 'Have you still got that sweet little Chinese boy?'

'Yes,' I said. 'Feng.'

'And what about that nutter, what was his name?' I'd seen her last quite soon after Cal arrived.

'Cal. Yeah, he's still here.'

'Did he turn out like you thought, like that David?' We had a child once before a bit like Cal, with the same sort of behavioural difficulties, but much older, older than me. Amy remembers him well because he was the one who threw a stone at her, which was also when her parents stopped her coming round to ours.

'A bit. But he's only six so it doesn't matter as much.'

'You know, my friend at school, Ellie, asked me about my scar,' she said. The scar is mostly under her hairline so it's not that noticeable. 'She couldn't believe someone just chucked a rock at me. They all think it's completely, like, amazing, that my best friend at home lives in a foster family and has all these disturbed kinds of kids in the house.' She said it companionably, not to be nasty, but I didn't feel like being polite or nice or pretending I felt all right about it.

'Wow,' I said. 'I bet they all think you're really street.'

'I didn't mean that. I meant, all the people at my school live in such a bubble . . . '

'And you don't.'

'Not as much, no,' she said, offended. 'Sorry. I didn't mean to upset you. You know I like your family, at least the ones who don't throw rocks at me.'

There was a gap. 'Right, yeah,' I said. 'Sorry.'

We watched one of our favourite films, *Jesus Christ Superstar*, that we must have watched about a hundred times together, but it wasn't the same. I got sleepy and it was very hard trying to think of things to say. I wanted to be at home where you could shout at someone and it would be OK, and where time filled up with things and conversations that were either easy or necessary. So after dinner, which was nice because it was moussaka, which we don't have at home, I left. I said I had revision to do, which was true, of course.

I couldn't sleep that night. There was a draught blowing under Adam's door because of the open window, so I slipped in to close it as much as I could without making it impossible for him to get in from the outside. Raindrops were just beginning to blow against the windowpane, and the sill was wet. I dried it off with my nighty so Adam wouldn't slip if he had to come in for some reason.

I lay awake for what felt like hours, and it was too, I think. In the end I needed the toilet, and on my way back I went into Adam's room again. I only meant to have a peek out of the window and see if the light in the shed was on, which it wasn't, but I ended up pushing open the window. The rain blew in my face so I stopped long enough to pull on one of his jumpers that was hanging off the back of his chair, then I scrambled out into the wet tree.

I was soaking when I got to the shed, and I woke them both up – Adam nearly had a heart attack, but he went straight back to sleep when I said I'd give her a bottle. Afterwards I squished up on the other side of the basket and settled down. Then I had no problem sleeping.

In the half-light when morning was coming, the baby threatened to cry, so I took her and her panda and her little flat mattress out of the basket and shoved the basket onto the red chair, so that she could lie between us and I could put my arm over her. She kept making all these little whimpers and wriggles that kept me awake, though Adam was still asleep. I'd put her down facing me. Her eyes were half shut, but her mouth was open in a triangle shape like it always was, except when she was screaming. She was wriggling and wriggling, and I sort of realised even though I was nearly asleep that she was getting closer and closer to me. So I watched her, and as she got nearly close enough to touch my face I worried that maybe she'd mistaken my nose for a bottle and she was going to be all disappointed, but instead, when she was resting with her mouth against my cheek, she stopped wriggling and went back to sleep.

Chapter Seven

I'd barely seen Dad that week with all the time we were spending in the shed, but he'd said he was coming round on Friday after work to really get some revision done with me. While Mum was getting dinner ready that evening she asked me if I'd mind just taking Cal to the park for a run; it had rained all day so he hadn't had any outside time, even at school, and he was going mad. It had stopped raining now and the sky was getting pale over towards the park. She said it would do me good to have a break, after studying with Adam and before studying with Dad. I said OK. Feng had a cold so he stayed behind.

Cal didn't want to go out, like always, and walked most of the way sideways-on to me with his back to the walls we were passing as if I was a wild beast, but as usual he was in a much better mood by the time we got there. He ran straight across the grass to the playground. Cal can stay for hours on the swings if he's allowed, it's one thing he really likes, and you have to watch him if there's already someone else on them because he will start trying to get them off. But no one was anywhere near so I left him to it.

I felt all tired and dreamy again, and wandered off the path towards the trees, but not too close because they were still dripping. The trees there are enormous tall evergreens, very dark, and standing underneath them is a bit like being in a cathedral or something. Dad lost a ball in one of them once, years and years ago, because it got lodged between branches so high up; we used to look for it whenever we passed, but you can't see it anymore.

As I stared up there was a rainbow. Rainbows are so strange; there are so many pictures of them, and books and TV programmes are full of them but you hardly ever actually see one. And even when you do, and even when it's really bright, it's nothing like the ones you see in pictures.

So I stood there gaping at this watery wash of colours on the sky, as if I had nothing in the world I should be doing, till I heard shouting and chains rattling and looked round, and Cal was still on the swing but there was a bunch of other boys around him. With Cal that was alarming. I should have stayed near him. You can tell when a bunch is nasty, and there were no adults anywhere near, or other kids either. I took off at a run but I can't run very fast. By the time I got to the playground gate I had a killer stitch.

I used to go to the school Cal goes to and I knew the boys who were round him now, especially one called Ryan who's the brother of Lily Buckley in my class. They're all skinny in that family but he has kind of a narrow bullet head as well and I knew he had a big mouth. Cal had stopped the swing by the time I got near but was still holding on to one of the chains with both hands. There were four of them standing round, all much taller than he was in his little kid red cotton hoodie, laughing at him and calling him mad and a freak. I stumbled through the gate just as Cal jumped off the swing and slapped at one of them. They were all laughing still, and kind of shoving him a bit between them so that he staggered. I started shouting. I'm not very good at that kind of stuff, but I ran into the middle of them and got hold of Cal by his arm and his jacket and shouted at them. I asked them what the hell they were doing, picking on him like that. 'He's only six, what's wrong with you?' I said. They were all older than Cal, at least nine. Of course I was much bigger than them, but they didn't take any notice of me. They still kept laughing, and said he was the one who attacked them. One of them said he was a weirdo and a freak. 'They shouldn't let him out on his own.'

'Looked after,' another one of them said. 'He should be locked up.'

'You just leave him alone, Ryan Buckley,' I said, to the one I knew.

'All right, Fat Phoeb,' he said, and his mates nearly split their sides laughing, and I let go of Cal's hood and he head-butted Ryan Buckley in the chest and knocked him over. I think if you didn't know what was going on but had looked over at just that moment, like all the adults who were over the other side of the playground seemed to, it would have looked really violent. It certainly left Ryan Buckley looking a bit pathetic, groaning on his back, and one of his mates shoved Cal, who looked ready to go again, so I got hold of him and dragged him out, slithering him along the yellow railings, and up the first part of the road. After a while he stopped resisting me and let me hold his wrist and just walked along with me, because he noticed I was crying.

When we were nearly home and the street was quiet, I said to him, 'Do kids often do that, bait you like that?'

'Sometimes,' he said.

'Is that what happens at school? Is that why you fight, because people are picking on you?' He was always fighting at school. He'd got excluded from the last one, which was about the time they sent him to us.

'Sometimes.'

'You're not a freak, Cal. You've just got a problem with your attention, and your energy.'

'There's another kid in my class who has to take pills, I saw him,' he said. 'He doesn't get mad all the time, though.'

'Do you think you should be having pills?' I asked, wiping my nose. I didn't know if anyone had actually asked him before.

He shrugged. 'Even when I did have them I used to get mad.'

'Well, you know, a lot's happened to you, I suppose.' I'd heard Mum say that depression and anger often aren't signs that there's something wrong with a person, that sometimes they're the correct response to circumstances. I secretly used to expect that eventually our foster kids would stop being angry or sad or whatever because they'd realise that now they were with us all their problems were over. I knew better than that by now.

'Yeah. I wish they'd leave me alone, though.'

We walked along for a while whilst I thought what to say. In the end I just said, 'If you didn't fight, maybe they wouldn't pick on you.'

He didn't say anything to that. Instead, when we'd just got nearly to the front door, he said, 'If your dad doesn't come back, do you think I'll have to move as well?'

'What do you mean, Cal?'

'Will they let us stay if it's just Mum, Gillian, looking after us?' He stood there looking at me. He said, 'I mean, I know if they only let one of us stay, you'll all want Feng.'

He wasn't being accusing, just matter-of-fact. What I wanted to say was that we would never be able to choose between him and Feng, and that anyway of course they'd both be staying with us, but Mum and Dad always said we shouldn't lie to Cal, at least not with things about him, because trust was a big problem for him. In fact, they'd always said to be careful not to be pulled into this kind of conversation.

So I just said, 'I don't know, Cal. But I want you both to stay,' and then I opened the front door and we went in.

There was a bit of a funny atmosphere that evening. Mum was running round in a bad temper trying to get the dinner on the table, and for the first time that week she was cross about Adam not coming to the table. 'Why does he keep hiding in the shed?' she muttered at me. 'Did we do something to him?' Also, she looked up across the table at me halfway through dinner when I was talking to Feng, and I knew she'd suddenly seen I'd been crying. She kept looking at me after that. But just as I was clearing the table and wondering how to run away before she could corner me, the doorbell went. Mum made Dad ring the bell now when he came round, if the rest of us were in, though he still had a key because it was him who brought Feng and Cal home from school.

When I opened the door, he wasn't there. He was standing outside the front-room window making faces at Feng, who was giggling through it. I couldn't be bothered to stand there like an idiot waiting for him to finish so I left the door open and headed back to the little room, but before I got there he stuck his head round the side of the door and said, 'It's me!' in a crazy accent. I think he thought he owed it to us to come in all cheerful and jolly now that he wasn't there all the time.

Anyway, Feng was glad to see him, and Cal came running up as if he didn't want to but couldn't help it. I didn't mind that they were all pleased to see each other, I honestly didn't, I wasn't jealous or anything. And I wasn't as angry with Dad as Adam was, nowhere near. But I felt a bit short-tempered. We all had a lot to cope with, and just then it felt like most of it was because of Dad not being around all the time.

So I wasn't as welcoming as they were, I just finished clearing the table and sat down at it to wait. After a while Mum swept the boys away and Dad sat down with me to do some maths and geography revision. Everyone in our family hates geography so Dad gets to help me with it. He ruffled my hair and hugged me and asked how school was, and I said it was OK and opened up my maths textbook. But it was terrible because I just couldn't force myself to concentrate and I couldn't do anything. I caught Dad looking at me as well. 'Are you all right, love?' he said.

'Yeah. Don't worry, I did some of this with Adam yesterday and I was fine,' I said.

'So how come you can't do it now?'

I thought I might cry again and I got up to get a drink. Dad came into the kitchen after me and I heard him mumble something to Mum, who was washing the dishes. She snapped back at him, 'No, she's not OK. Why should she be?'

Dad turned to me as I was standing there and said, 'You look exhausted, sweetheart.'

'She's not sleeping,' Mum said, slamming the baking tray down on the draining board.

'I'm sleeping fine,' I said. 'I might just go and get my other geography book from the shed.'

'Tell Adam to come and get his dinner,' Mum said.

'What's he doing in the shed, anyway?' Dad asked.

'They're not happy, Richie,' Mum said as I went off through the back door. I should have stayed to stop them both worrying and arguing, but I was too upset. I had to spend two minutes sniffling into the garden wall halfway between the house and the shed before I could go and get Adam.

Every now and again in the evenings, when the baby was asleep, we'd been trying to fit in twenty minutes when we were both in the house at the same time so Mum wouldn't notice she wasn't seeing us together at all, and so far the baby had still been asleep every time we went back. Adam used it that evening to pop in and scoff his dinner and have a kind of uncomfortable chat with Dad. Then he went back to the shed and Dad left.

The phone went just as we were saying goodbye to him in the hall and Mum answered it. A couple of minutes later, just as Cal and I were starting a row over what I was going to watch on TV while he got ready for bed, she came in looking stern and said Mrs Austin, who she knows from the primary school, had rung her up to tell her Cal had been in a fight at the playground and pushed some other child over. Mum wasn't surprised about that but she was surprised I hadn't told her. We all had to pull together when it came to helping Cal, she said, not tell tales, but keep each other in the loop.

'There was a bunch of kids picking on him,' I said.

'Where were you?' Mum asked suspiciously.

'I was just outside the playground, and by the time I got to him they were already winding him up.' I saw she wasn't going to let it go so I had to say, even though Cal was there, 'They were calling him names, saying he was mad and stuff.'

Mum looked all poker-faced. 'What did you do?'

'I told them to stop.'

'And?'

106

'They called Phoebe "Fat Phoeb",' Cal piped up. 'So I butted one of them.'

'Is that what happened?' she said to me and I had to nod. I would never have told her that if Cal hadn't. She got down on her knees and put her arms round Cal. 'Little bastards,' she said, and grabbed hold of me around the waist too. Feng was peering over the side of his chair, all anxious, so I sort of patted him on the hand.

We were all tired out by the whole thing. It was my night for the baby, and I knew I should pretend to go to bed so that Adam could come back in, but I also knew Mum would want to talk to me about it so I waited around till she'd turned the lights off for Feng and Cal and come downstairs. She made me tell her everything that I'd heard them say to Cal, which wasn't all that much. She said she'd have to go into the school and talk to the teachers about it, make sure they understood that he was being teased and provoked at least some of the time. We sat and worried together for a bit. I could have told her about Cal and Feng being all anxious about Dad being gone, but it felt like that would be too much for both of us that night, so I said I was going to bed.

'OK. You're not fat, you know that, don't you Phoebe?' she said suddenly as I was passing her on the way to the door.

'Oh yes,' I said, thinking that in that case it was strange

that everyone called me it. I didn't feel fat, in my head, till I saw my reflection somewhere and then it was worse than if I remembered it all the time. I was just a lump, that was all. Actually, I half thought I might get a bit thinner through all this, because underneath the big thick blanket of tiredness I was also always a bit hungry. I suppose it was being up and about for so much longer every day. Also, I didn't have any money to buy chocolate at school. Adam and I were saving up all the coins we could get our hands on for more nappies.

Saturday morning was sunny and warm again. Mum said Dad was going to help her do the shopping, because there was no way she could manage it on her own with Cal and Feng, and then Feng was going out with his mum for lunch, and she and Dad were going to take Cal for a picnic. Adam said she'd rung Dad last night and she was all strung out about poor Cal so they decided they had to pay him some attention together. They were leaving me at home to revise, and if I needed anything Adam would help me.

Adam said we should celebrate somehow because we'd had the baby a week now. It was hard to believe really, but in some ways it was even harder to believe it had only been that long. It was such a nice day, and for some reason we were both in really good moods so we decided to bring the baby out into the fresh air. The grass at the shed end of the garden was still wet because it doesn't get the sun till afternoon, so we spread the fleecy blanket out near the house. The back door was open so that we could hear if by any chance Mum and Dad came back freakishly early. We put her on the blanket and kept her mostly shaded from the sun with a huge stone flowerpot that had been sitting empty by the wall since we moved in. There were white roses blowing every-where, over all the walls, and big fat red tulips between the laurel bushes. I'd been trying to tell her a story; I'd sort of half-remembered one about a lost baby, but it was the wrong way round, with a princess thinking she was a shepherd's daughter and her real parents finding her when she grew up and taking her away to live a princessy life, and anyway when Adam brought some tea out I was too embarrassed to go on, so I sort of read my French vocabulary book.

'I wish we knew her birthday,' Adam said, chewing on a piece of grass from one of the small, damp clumps the mower had left behind.

'Why?' I said. 'Are you wondering how we'll throw her a first birthday party in the shed in a year's time?'

'No, smarty,' he said. 'But it feels wrong that she doesn't have one.'

'I can think of things that are wronger,' I said.

'I know.' He chomped the grass. 'Like her not being breastfed.'

'Ew, Adam. Not really.'

'Everyone says babies should be breastfed, that it's best for them.'

'Not if their mother's Leanne. Anyway, there's nothing we can do about that. Unless you want us to find her a whatdoyoucallit, a wet nurse, like Moses or someone.'

'Like Moses?'

'Yeah, you know after he got dumped in the bulrushes. I'm sure it says the pharaoh's daughter got him a wet nurse.'

'No, fool, the reason it mentions it is because it was his mother in disguise.'

'Well, anyway. I was thinking more of the fact she doesn't have a name.' We had avoided talking about it so far, I think because it was such a big thing.

'I know,' Adam said, frowning into his mug.

'It feels like staking a big claim, though, doesn't it. But she's not some kind of lost orphan.'

'Well, she is.'

'She's got us.'

'That's true,' he said. 'We're the best she's got.'

'I think we should call her something,' I said.

He sat up. 'Good. So do I. Good, that can be our one-week celebration, naming her. But let's make it a good name. An appropriate one.'

'Like what?'

'Look, she's a baby who lives in a garden. That's, you know, significant. We must be able to think of something. There's Rose, of course.'

'Not Rose, there are too many of them.' I leaned over the baby, who was awake and looking at her feet. 'You're not a Rose, are you, darling? You need a name of your own, don't you?'

'Ivy? That grows on sheds.'

'Yeah, but no one likes it, Adam, and it pulls walls down.'

Adam said, showing off, 'Perdita means "lost" in Latin, it would be sort of appropriate.' I'd known that already, actually, from *101 Dalmatians*, but I didn't bother saying so.

'No, that's a sad name. She should have a happy one.' I thought of one that made my chest swell up, it was so good. 'Iris.'

'Iris?' Adam looked around. 'Do we have irises?' Even he knows what irises look like because they're Mum's favourite flower, and Dad used to bring her some from the flower shop every now and then.

'No, not because of the flower. She was the goddess of the rainbow.'

'How do you know that?' Adam is always amazed when I know things, especially when it's from school, which I told him this was. As a matter of fact, when Mum and

111

I used to go to the library after school for stories, when I was little, there was a man there who told stories from Greek myths, and I remembered it from that.

'It's good,' I said. 'Rain and sunshine mixing together, the sky and all that.' I picked the baby up and told her, 'Your name's Iris.' She poked me in the eye with her fist.

I changed her nappy, and Adam read her another story, and we drank more tea and gave Iris some milk – it was funny how much she was Iris already – and then Adam went to sleep and I put my head down next to her and blew on her cheek. Then I think we fell asleep too, or at least I did, on the rug with my legs sticking into the sun. Because the next thing I heard were voices coming round the corner of the house.

So there we were, sprawling on a blanket with a baby no one in the world knew existed except us and Leanne, as far as we knew. The shed was too far to bolt to; even the corner where the garden bends was too far, because we'd sat deliberately close to the house – we'd meant to hear anyone coming in. How could we have known whoever it was wouldn't have keys and would be coming round to the back? I was sure we'd have heard the doorbell if they'd rung it.

Adam was quicker than me, as usual. He grabbed the baby, so fast she didn't even squeak, and flew in the back door, nearly falling up the step. All I could do was flip the corner of the blanket over the nappy that had been lying there. I couldn't see how we were getting out of it, not with the baby in the house; just as we'd been settling into it and given her a name. There was a bit of a squeak of wheels and a laugh, and Feng came round the corner with his chair being pushed by his mother.

Feng's mother is Chinese and she hardly speaks any English. She seems to love Feng a lot, and I'm not quite sure why he couldn't live with her, but he hasn't since he was two or three. I once asked Mum about it and she said some people have great troubles coping, however much they want to, and that everyone's built differently with different strengths. Feng saw her quite often, every few weeks, anyway, but she didn't come round to the house very much.

It must have looked a bit weird, me lying there, not even in the sun, obviously half asleep with two empty mugs and a couple of books scattered about. I sat up and tried to be friendly, but I'm not much good at chatting. They'd come back early because she had some kind of appointment and the café where they went for lunch had been so crowded they would have had to wait for ages, so they'd given up. Apparently they had tried ringing the doorbell, so that was a lesson for us on how much to trust our ears. She had a quick cuddle with Feng, and made him tell me to look after him and take him in if he got cold, or hot. I couldn't exactly send her back round the corner, so I saw her through the house and to the front door with panting politeness. Adam was obviously hidden upstairs by now. I wondered how I could persuade Feng to go and sit in the front room with a blanket over his head while we smuggled the baby back out. His mother had lifted him onto the rug before she left, luckily onto the far end where there were no nappies hidden. He was flipping the pages of Adam's physics book over.

'Where's Adam?'

'Inside,' I said airily. 'Fancy watching some TV?'

'Nah.'

'Hungry?'

'I can wait till the others get back.'

'OK,' I said desperately. Any minute now the baby would be crying. 'Do you – er – do you want to do some reading?'

He looked up at me with his shiny eyes and solemn face. 'Phoebe.'

'Mmm?'

'What's going on?'

'What do you mean?' I moved from one foot to another, thinking of just running into the house to get away from the conversation.

'I know something is. You've hardly been in the house, and nor has Adam, and you both look really...'

'Shifty?' I said, and laughed.

He nodded. 'Shifty, the whole time. And you fall asleep whenever you sit down. And you haven't read with me all week. I finished the *Dr Seuss* books—'

'Well done!'

He looked at me reproachfully. 'You haven't even properly spoken to me in ages, or to any of us. I know you don't want me to know, so I tried not to notice, but I'm worried. And Cal's worried too.'

'Is he?'

'You know he looks like he's about to burst, worse than usual, and no one's noticing. No one's talking to him except me. No one talks about anything at the moment,' he added sadly.

I could have just left him there for a bit, till I'd recovered. Or I could have had some presence of mind and sat down next to him and let him tell me about Cal, or himself, or what he thought about Mum and Dad, or I could just have fobbed him off with some kind of reassuring rubbish. But I didn't have the stomach for it somehow. There I'd been, congratulating myself for taking such good care of the baby, keeping the secret so well and protecting her from the rest of the world who might try to take her away from me, but I hadn't fooled an eight-year-old. I dropped down beside Feng and looked at the sky and told him about the baby.

I hadn't got very far into the story, in fact, I hadn't got past the obvious opening statement, when he interrupted and said he didn't believe me. Not so much in a challenging way but as if he really didn't believe me, and wondered what I was playing at. So that was another chance for me to change tack, but I didn't. I carried on and he looked at me with his eyes getting bigger. 'But where did you get her? Where is she now?'

I stood up and shouted for Adam. After a few seconds he opened his bedroom window above us and leaned out. I could tell he was trying to look all jolly. 'What's up? Hi, Feng.'

'Bring her down,' I shouted, feeling a bit lightheaded as if I'd stood up too quick. 'Bring Iris down.'

If he'd been near enough I'm sure he would have hit me. I've never seen him frown like that. 'What are you talking about? What have you done?'

'I told Feng,' I said. 'He knew. He knew there was something. He did, Adam.'

'You didn't have to tell him what! Oh, *bloody* hell,' he hissed, and disappeared. I sat down next to Feng again.

'You did know.'

'Yes,' he soothed me.

A moment later Adam appeared, still frowning, marching out with the baby bundled up on his shoulder. She was awake but she had her glazed look on. 'I don't

116

know what you were thinking,' he announced, slinging her down between us. 'You've gone mad.'

'I know,' I said. 'Sorry.'

'Right, Feng,' he said, with his hands on his hips, 'this probably seems a bit strange, but keep an open mind.'

'OK,' said Feng, holding out his finger to the baby.

'What exactly have you told him?' Adam asked me. 'Well, Feng, she got left. Did you tell him who . . . ?'

'Yeah – who?' Feng interrupted, without looking at either of us. He was enthralled with Iris. She looked much better than she had a week ago, when we first saw her. Her skin was smoothing out and she looked less like a bundle, as well as being cleaner.

'By someone who wanted Mum and Dad to keep her.' I could see Adam wanted to hang onto any shred of the secret he could, but I couldn't see the point, and I didn't want to have to set up another big frame of lies. Since Feng was in on the story it was obviously easier for him to know the whole of it.

'Leanne,' I said. 'She used to live here, for a bit. We found her in the shed last Saturday.'

'Last Saturday!'

'Yes, we've kept her a week,' Adam said proudly, and kicked me on the leg.

'Iris, he means, the baby,' I explained, rubbing my shin. 'Leanne left the same night and we haven't seen her since.'

'She said she wasn't coming back. She said she wanted Mum and Dad to have the baby because she didn't want her, but she didn't want her to go into Care, either.'

'No,' agreed Feng at once.

'But we thought that Mum and Dad might not be allowed, especially with Dad not being at home at the moment,' Adam went on, 'so we thought we'd try and hang on to her for a little while and see what happens. We figured the longer we keep her, the more chance it gives Mum and Dad to sort things out, and maybe if we've looked after her for a while already, they might be more likely to let her stay here.'

Feng was only eight. He didn't question it. But hearing it out loud made me think what I hadn't for a few days – that it was pretty weak and it didn't make much sense. We'd made ourselves want to keep her, but of course we hadn't been doing anything that would make them let us. I could tell from the way Adam's voice had died away that he was thinking it too.

We all sat quietly for a bit. I think Feng was a bit overcome, which was understandable, but after a while he got the giggles. He rolled over on his side and hooted. Iris lay there staring at him. She was still holding his finger. I caught Adam smiling.

We couldn't relax for very long. It wasn't safe even for Feng to stay out in the garden any longer, since if Cal saw him he'd be sure to want to play out too. Adam had taken the baby into the shed and nipped back out to help me get Feng in. 'So now I can help!' he said as we eased him up the back step. I didn't know what to say. Sometimes it was like Feng forgot he couldn't walk. 'I mean, I can help distract them, especially if you both have to be out in the shed. I can think of stuff to tell them.'

'That would be good,' I agreed. 'You're great at distractions.' He could even distract Cal from himself sometimes.

Chapter Eight

I could see there were new problems now that Feng knew. I'd just proved it was easy to blow it, and now there were three of us who might. Besides, now there were also three of us needing to talk sometimes and that was just much more noticeable, especially as Feng couldn't get about very easily. And especially as the only one who was left out now, and who had lots of time to watch us all, was Cal.

We didn't have to worry about him for that day, because he was so happy when he got back from the picnic. Dad came in for a while and while Mum was getting him to fix the sagging window in the front room, Cal shoved me out into the kitchen where Feng was to tell us that they'd had a really good time. 'They did! They hardly argued at all and when they did it was friendly! And look...' He had a whole lot of photos to show us on the camera. Cal places an awful lot of importance on photographs. Mum and Dad have always believed it's a really big deal to get pictures of us all as a family in our different incarnations, so we've got albums, not to mention walls, bursting with snaps of all the kids who've stayed with us, even those who were only here a couple of weeks; but we've never had a kid who got so into it as Cal. I think he was really impressed when Mum said that every child who's been a part of the family stays as part of the family for ever. It had never occurred to him that he'd met hardly any of them since he'd been here.

So we had to look at a raft of photos of Mum and Dad and Cal, which we were glad to do to keep him in a good mood, but Feng kept giving me big significant looks, and I was thinking that should have known things were too simple to last. So I went upstairs to have a nap before Cal started sniffing the air to find out what he was being left out of, or Dad wanted to do some revision with me, or Mum wanted to know what Adam was doing.

I didn't realise just how nervous Adam was, and how annoyed he was with me, till that evening when we crossed over in the shed. I'd decided it was quite nice Feng knowing. Although he was only eight, I thought he was a pretty safe person to tell, and though it gave us more problems, it meant there was someone else who could help as well. But Adam was furious and started on me as soon as the door shut. 'I really can't believe what you did, by the way,' he said. 'I think it was utterly stupid and selfish of you. Just so you know.'

I started getting worked up too. I'm not very good at standing up for myself, except sometimes, when I feel like I might be to blame. 'I think you're overreacting.'

'Oh, you do.' He stood up. 'Just to make yourself feel better, you've completely endangered what we've been doing here. Endangered Iris.'

'Feng knew something was up. He'd have started watching us even more . . .'

'Because we couldn't have got past an eight-year-old in a wheelchair. Don't give me that, you just wanted to spill it to someone. And now you've risked all this, never mind the responsibility you've put on Feng, because you just couldn't be bothered. You just flaked out.'

'Well, I'm tired,' I burst out, almost tearfully. 'I'm really tired.'

'Yeah. I'm tired too. Look, Phoebe, I know you're younger than me. But you can't be all – young – over this because it's important.'

'I know it's bloody important! It's too bloody important!' I shouted at him. My nose was running. 'And don't come at me with your reverse psychology. I know I'm young and it's true, I can't handle it, and neither can you.'

'So what do you want to do?' he shouted back at me. 'Just give her up?' He flailed his arm at Iris, who was lying in her basket with her eyes all unfocused. 'Ship her off to the children's home?'

'They might not,' I said. 'And we can't just keep her here for ever, you know we can't.'

'Not if you go telling everyone.'

'Oh, so if I hadn't told Feng you'd have been planning to keep her in the shed till, what, her eighteenth birthday?'

Adam sat down and rubbed his eyes. 'We've got to hang on as long as we can.'

'Why? If it's not going to make any difference in the long run?' There were tears sliding down the sides of my face, but they were coming on their own. I was too tired to cry properly.

'Because things might get better. We don't know what's going to happen. And if we give up now, it's as bad as it can possibly be. There's no way Mum will be allowed to keep her. And do you have any idea, have you given any thought to what we'd get if we went in with her now and said, "Oh, we've just kept her in the garden for a week like a sick bird"? An anonymous child that no one in the world even knows exists?' His voice was flat, but I had a kind of flash then of exactly the kind of trouble it would be, and how unforgiveable it would seem for us to have played a game like this with a real baby.

'What you'd get, you mean,' I screamed at him. 'You're the oldest and this was all your stupid idea.'

Iris started crying and because Adam was just sitting against the wall with his head in his hands, I went to pick her up, and plug her into the bottle that had been cooling. She snuggled up against my arm. I thought about what it would be like if she was taken away, and I looked across at Adam. He hadn't moved. 'I won't tell anyone else,' I said after a while. 'Don't worry about Feng, he won't tell anyone, and we don't have to let him be drawn in, either. If we can make it work for just a bit longer maybe they won't think we were just being totally irresponsible. If we stick with it a bit.'

'It's not just the trouble we might get into, or I might,' he said from between his hands. 'It's not even just Iris anymore. I don't know what Social Services would make of it, you know. Mum and Dad might be in trouble too. I don't know what would happen with Feng and Cal—'

'All right,' I said. 'I said all right.'

The next day was Sunday and Dad wasn't working so he'd wanted to take us all out for lunch and a walk after swimming, but of course someone had to get out of it to stay with Iris. It was much easier for me because of my exams starting the next day, but I had to make a big song and dance out of how nice it would be to have the house to myself so that Mum would go out too. She'd half-planned to go into town shopping with her friend Daphne that she used to work with, so we all encouraged her heavily to stick to it. I knew if she was there I'd be risking her bringing me tea and chocolate biscuits in the shed to keep me going. She'd already said she felt guilty for not being able to help me revise more. Dad joined in too, because he said she deserved a break. Cal sat looking at us all with his eyebrows nearly resting on his cheeks, and I could see trouble brewing there, but he didn't say anything. I think we should probably have told Feng to leave it to us; it was bad enough me and Adam suddenly caring about Mum having a chance to buy some new tights.

I know what I'd been saying just the night before to Adam, but I was glad to get a chance to spend some time on my own with Iris because I'd have to go to school every day that week. Adam had even been saying I should sleep in my bedroom most of the nights otherwise my exams might be so bad someone would notice. I'd said no; things were getting a bit funny between me and Adam, with both of us trying to prove how serious we were about looking after her properly. But actually once I was on my own it was gloomy. The baby was asleep but I couldn't concentrate on revision. The rain was spattering down again outside, and I kept switching between feeling sweaty and feeling a bit chilly. Then I got worried in case I was getting ill, because I'd woken up that morning with a sniffle. Mum had said I'd probably caught Feng's cold. In one way it would have been nice to get out of exams but I couldn't possibly actually be ill, because then Mum or Dad would have to stay off work to look after me, plus Mum would ring up school to tell them and someone might mention that I'd been off three days last week too. So I had a bit of a panic, but then it stopped raining and there was a gleam of sunlight across the ceiling of the shed, and I stopped feeling ill and tried to learn my French.

When Iris woke up I was fed up with the shed so I took her inside the house and gave her some things to hold, like wooden spoons and a silk scarf Mum had left hanging over the stairs, and I played her some music in the front room that we both liked. It was nice to have a bit of space and time to play; I wanted to make it up to her, for what I'd said when I was arguing with Adam. I felt sick about having said we should give her up. We sat on the sofa for her bottle, propped against the big cushions, with the TV on, and for a moment I was thinking how easy it was to look after a baby if you didn't have to keep her in a shed. But then she started squirming and crying just before the programme ended, and she wouldn't settle and I couldn't do any more work. I felt really tired, and the thought of

126

having to go to school the next day and start a week of exams was miserable.

I'd flip flopped again and all I really wanted to do was go up to my room, by myself, and shut the door and shut the curtains and put music on too loud to hear anything outside the room, and maybe sleep, but I couldn't do that so I traipsed into the garden with her. It was really sunny now, and all the wetness on the branches and the grass was glittering too bright to look at, and there was a hot smell of sodden grass and bushes. I went back inside and upstairs and pinched Mum's orange rain slicker out of her cupboard, then went back to our part of the garden and spread it on the grass for Iris to lie on. I got my shorts soaking wet straight away from sitting next to her.

'Whose baby is that?'

I flung my head back and nearly toppled onto Iris. I didn't even have time to panic like I had when Feng and his mum were coming round the corner. Almost over the top of our heads, lying on a branch of the tree whose shade Iris was in and that looked far too delicate to support him, there was a boy. He was laughing down at me; I could see his teeth in the gloom of the tree.

'Sorry,' he said. 'Didn't mean to scare you.'

'Yes, you did,' I said crossly, 'or you would have coughed or something.'

He giggled. 'What's your name?'

'Phoebe,' I said, since it's not much use pretending to be someone you're not when you're sitting in your own garden. I knew who he was, actually, he went to my school. Funnily enough I'd known who he was for years, because he'd taken the scholarship exams for Adam's school at the same time as Adam, and once Adam started we'd found out that he'd come second in it, which was meant to be brilliant, and this boy, Kiran he was called, had come first. So Adam had a thing about him, only then after a year he'd left, and obviously gone to my school instead because there he was when I started secondary. I recognised him straight away. He had very clear skin, like glossy toffee if you hold it up to a lamp, and thick shiny hair with a side parting, and white teeth. Of course I would have known who he was by now anyway; he was one of those people that everyone knows, though I'd never spoken to him. I'd seen him in the streets around and about where we lived a handful of times; he'd helped Mum off a bus once with Feng's wheelchair, but I hadn't realised his was the house whose garden backed onto ours. Everything was an odd shape around here and I couldn't figure out even now what street his house would be on.

'I'm Kiran,' he said, and moved. He seemed to be preparing to swing down.

'You're not coming down here,' I said, alarmed.

'Oh, am I not? Sorry.' He lay back down. 'Who's the baby?'

'Iris.' I was sweating again. I wished Adam was there, so he could see how this wasn't my fault. Too much had gone on this weekend. I was supposed to be learning French.

'Nice. But who is she? I mean, whose is she?'

'Ours,' I said, trying to sound surprised by the question.

He raised his eyebrows. They were so thick and dark I could see them, even though I was looking up into the shade of the tree. 'I didn't know your mum was having a baby.'

'How would you know?' He was very puzzling, which another time I might have liked, but I could have done without it now.

'Oh, I've seen her out and about with you and a parcel of kids.'

'You must be very observant,' I said primly.

He grinned. 'Yeah, I am. And I saw you in the play last year. So when I saw you with all those little boys I recognised you.'

'Yes, well, they're my foster brothers. And Iris,' I held her up to him, 'is my foster sister.'

'Oh, right. You keep her in the garden a lot, don't you?'

My stomach dropped into my bottom and I think I must have gone pale or something because he looked concerned, as much as he could while he was lying in a tree.

'Sorry, it's just come up here quite a lot. And I've seen you, and your brother, out here. I haven't been perving or anything, or listening to your conversations. But I've heard the baby cry a couple of times.'

'It's my little brother,' I said as rapidly as I could. 'My foster brother, I mean. He doesn't like the baby much, he's jealous, you know, he's a bit needy, got issues, and so my mum sometimes gets us to bring Iris out here so she can pay Cal a bit of attention, you see. Or sometimes she brings her out,' I added. 'My mum, that is, you must just not have seen her.'

'Right,' he said. 'Oh well, you've got a nice garden. Do you never take her out, out of the house?'

I think he was just making conversation, but I was very nervous. 'No, well, we don't have a pushchair for her yet. We haven't had her long you see, only a week, and my parents haven't had a chance to get everything they need. We didn't get much warning about her.'

'Oh, that's great! I've got a pushchair!'

'What?'

He was wriggling backwards on his branch. 'We've got a pushchair we've been dying to get rid of. My sister's outgrown it, she's nearly four now, and we just never use it, and my mum's been threatening for ages to make me walk it down to the tip or something, only she keeps thinking that we'll find someone to give it to.'

'No,' I called desperately as he started disappearing down the tree trunk, on his side of the wall. 'No, I couldn't.'

'It's fine, it's in good condition and everything,' he said. I couldn't see him anymore but I could hear that he was still moving away. 'I'm sure it'll be useful, at least till your parents have the chance to get a new one. I'll get it right now and bring it round.'

'No,' I said. My voice sounded weak. It was too late, he'd gone. Iris was wide awake and beginning to whinge a bit and I couldn't possibly leave her there alone. All I could do was scoop her up and race into the house to the front door and pray that he would have come and gone before anyone came home; in fact, in time for me to have hidden a socking great pushchair as well as Iris in the shed before anyone came home.

I waited by the hall window, wondering how he knew where we lived, hopping up and down in a panic and really needing to go to the toilet, for absolutely ages. Of course, it probably wasn't really ages, he was probably quite quick at getting the pushchair from wherever it was in his house and sorting it out and bringing it round. When I saw him coming I laid Iris down on the carpet and darted out to grab it from him and haul it up the front step. 'Thank you so much,' I said, 'that's really kind.'

'No, honestly, we wanted to get rid of it . . .'

'I'd ask you in, but the rest of the family's not here at the moment and my mum would go nuts if I did,' I said. 'Sorry.'

'It's fine,' he said. 'You're on your own with the baby?'

'It's not for long. They'll be back really soon. I'd better get back to her,' I said, trying not to look round and give away the fact that the baby was lying on the hall floor behind the front door.

He gestured at the pushchair. 'Do you not want me to show you how to collapse it?'

'Oh, thanks,' I said, inventing wildly, 'my brother's a mechanical genius, I'm sure he'll figure it out.'

'OK then. See you around.'

'Bye!' I sang. I'm sure I sounded terrified. I shut the door, looked from the pushchair to the baby for a second, trying to decide which to hide first, then galloped with the stupid chair across the hall, through the kitchen, lugged it up the slope of the garden to just round the corner, then ran back. The furrows the wheels had made on the wet grass looked like someone had been dirt bike riding in our garden. There were wet wheel marks all across the kitchen floor too, and on the hall carpet, which was here when we moved in and isn't the cleanest but is still pale enough to show where a pushchair has been through off a wet street. There were little bits of light blossom crushed against the marks in some places. I guessed the rain must have scattered a lot of flower petals outside.

I grabbed Iris up so I could run if I heard anyone coming, whipped a tea towel from the kitchen and started scrubbing at all the marks I could see. I kept getting glimpses of my round pink face in the hall mirror. The baby nearly squirmed out of my arms, and the sweat was trickling off my nose onto the floor; then by the time I got back in the kitchen the light was different, or the marks were mostly dried, and I couldn't see where they were, so I ended up rubbing the cloth over most of the kitchen floor and probably making it dirtier than it had been, but finally I threw the towel in the washing machine and escaped up the garden to the shed. Of course then the others weren't back for almost an hour, but at least that gave my heart a chance to stop thumping.

Chapter Nine

'No way,' Adam was saying. He had his palms pressed tight against the sides of his head and his eyes shut. 'No way, Phoebe.'

'Yes. He offered us the pushchair. I didn't have a chance to stop him, and anyway I couldn't think of any reason why not, not straight off the bat like that.'

'What's happening? This is mad. We were fine for a week, and then yesterday, and now today...'

'It's OK,' I said soothingly.

'It's very much not OK. Are you mad? It's out of control.'

'No, Adam, it's not.'

'We don't even know this guy.'

'And that's what saves us, because now he knows we're a foster family, he thinks she's being fostered by us. By Mum and Dad. So everything's fine, everything's accounted for. The worst we've got to worry about is that

134

we can't wee in the garden anymore in case he's in the bloody tree.' I giggled, but my brain kept turning in a sort of groove of fascination from the horror of imagining that he might have seen me doing that already, to the fact that he'd seen me in the play last year and remembered me.

Adam was pacing up and down. 'And he didn't think it was the least bit odd that we were keeping her in a shed?'

'It's a summerhouse, remember, and I think he probably did think it was a bit strange, but I explained it, and he doesn't know we're actually *keeping* her there.'

'But what if he keeps coming back to the tree? He's going to figure it out, isn't he, that Iris is always there and Mum never is.'

'I don't think he will come back to the tree,' I said. 'I think I probably scared him off by being so weird.' And fat.

'I hope so, I really do. But God, he knows where we live and everything, he knows who you are … This is so bad. Potentially this is so bad.'

I knew he was right, but apart from the very self-centred things I couldn't get my brain off, it had been so sweet banging the door of the shed behind me and knowing I'd dodged a bullet again that I was happy. Besides, though it was scary, and it was, it was also quite nice that a few other people knew Iris existed, knew her name even, even if that was all they knew. I'd felt proud of her, I'd liked introducing her. 'How was the swimming and everything?'

His face changed expression. 'Well, funny you should ask. It was very weird.'

'Why?' I was alarmed.

'We were in the pool, and that was all right as usual, though Cal had a bit of a schiz when they opened it up for everyone else and we had to get out, but he was OK by the time we were all ready because of going for lunch. We just went to the café at the pool, you know.'

'Right.'

'And Cal was OK, actually, he was surprisingly fine. Didn't even spill anything, but then we were just waiting for the ice cream when this woman comes up to talk to us.'

'What woman?'

'I don't know. A friend of Dad's, he said. Called Antoinette, would you believe. She said she'd just come for a swim, but I don't know, Dad looked completely mortified. He tried to get us to leave straight away, I think he'd forgotten about the ice cream, and then Cal started getting in a state, and Dad more or less told this woman to go away and leave us alone. Coming home was ridiculous. Cal was punching windows all the way. In fact, you should go in really, or we might find he's murdered Dad and Feng.'

We sat in silence for a while. Iris was lying on Adam's lap, looking up at him. She could see further now. 'What did she look like?'

'I don't know. Tall, yellow hair, a bit scraggy.'

'Was she good-looking?'

'No,' he said loyally.

I trailed back up to the house to say hello to Dad, thinking it over and wondering what to say to Cal about it, but as it happened I didn't have to because there was already an almighty row going on. Mum had got back while I was out in the shed with Adam and the baby, and had just been putting her shopping bags on the table when one of the boys must have told her about this woman. Now she was kicking off at Dad. 'What the hell, Richie.'

'I know, honestly...'

'What was in your mind, just tell me that?'

'I had nothing to do with it,' I heard Dad say as I collected Feng from the kitchen and wheeled him through into the sitting room. 'Look, I'm sorry, I just happened to mention at work that I was taking the kids for lunch after swimming today. I never thought she'd turn up, I don't know what she was thinking.'

'I always told you she was fixated on you,' Mum shouted as I went back in for Cal, who was whacking one of the wooden chairs with a giant metal truck. 'Clearly now she thinks she's got a chance with you, why does she think that, Richie?'

'It's all right,' I said to them as I shut the sitting-room door. 'They'll have a row, then it'll be over.'

'No, it won't,' Cal said, quiet and savage. I thought

about giving him a hug but he would have hit me with his truck and it had sharp edges, so I gave Feng one instead.

'It might be a good thing,' I said. 'At least they're both angry with the same person, as well as with each other.'

'They're supposed to be going out tonight,' Feng said sadly. After Dad moved out, Mum and Dad started off going out once a week, just the two of them, so they'd have some time to themselves to talk, I suppose, but it hadn't happened for two weeks because Mum said she just didn't want to see his stupid face. She said the stupid part to the hall mirror, she didn't know I was still listening.

Cal was in a real temper and I was torn between letting him play on his DS or playing on the Wii with him, which I hadn't had time to do in ages, but while I was hovering Dad stomped past without even saying goodbye and the front door slammed, and that sent Cal into the stratosphere.

Mum was in a horrible mood as well but she couldn't just stay in the kitchen and bark at the knives and forks like she would have liked; she had to come out and deal with Cal because when he's like that he's beyond me. She carted him off to his room where there wasn't much left to break besides the window, and left me with Feng. Poor Feng, he would have loved to go out and see the baby, but quite clearly this wasn't the time to be doing new things and hoping no one would notice. I told him about Kiran. He was a bit put out that he hadn't got to be the newest person in the secret for very long, but I pointed out Kiran didn't know he was in it.

Adam had the baby that night. I only got to see her for a few minutes in the morning before I went to school, and Adam was wondering if we could somehow wangle Feng out of school one day that week because I had to go in every day for my exams, and he'd already missed two days himself. I worried about him sometimes, I really did. He'd got me all twined up in his plan so I couldn't bear to think of losing Iris either now, but he kept getting one step madder. I said there was no chance, either of us being able to spirit Feng out of school with no one noticing, or of me agreeing to leave the baby all day with an eight-year-old boy who couldn't even run for help in an emergency; he'd just have to bin off his posh school and his top marks for a week and put up with it. He quietened down and I had to head off to school but it stressed me out that little bit more.

School was a bit muted, with it being the first morning of exam week. Everyone was sitting around the edges of classrooms looking into the air and gabbling under their breath, or walking round the corridors with their heads stuck between book pages. Charlotte had hysterics before registration because she said she couldn't remember a single word of vocab; we had French first thing, which was just as well for me because I was a bit perkier in the mornings, and English in the afternoon, which would be easier. Not that anything was easy at the moment. I felt like I could sleep for a hundred years just sitting in one of those chairs with my head on the desk.

French was a disaster. I'd learned all those words over and over last week in the shed, and actually I remembered a lot of them, they kept floating into my head in the most useless way, but I couldn't string them together at all. In the oral part Mrs Lee was looking at me in a very odd way. I'm never very good at French, I'm always a bit slow, but I'm normally conscientious and I tend to know the grammar. Also, I usually get really embarrassed during orals, especially if I make a mistake, but I couldn't bring myself to care very much today.

I spent all lunchtime watching Marika pat Charlotte on the shoulder. Charlotte doesn't do well in exams, and she minds it.

English went better because you can float off on a cloud in an English exam and still be doing OK, but I wasn't in a great mood going home because I kept thinking that I had a whole four days still to go and no more English papers.

Mum made me go on and on about the exams, even though I didn't want to tell her and she didn't really want to hear. Cal was lying behind the sofa in the front room, which is a terrible sign, and even Feng was quieter than

140

usual. I went out to the shed as soon as I could and Adam was in a rotten mood. I think day after night after day in there was beginning to get to him. 'I almost cracked and took her out in that stupid pushchair today. It's just a temptation. And it takes up half the floor.'

'Put it outside then,' I snapped at him.

'How did your exams go?'

'Not very well.'

'Why not?'

'Er. Because I haven't had time to learn anything.'

'That's rubbish. You've had nothing but time to learn stuff, loads more than usual, in here with nothing else to do, up in the middle of the night.'

'I did try propping my book open on the table,' I admitted, 'but Iris always seems to know I'm not paying her full attention and starts squirming and screaming more.'

'What do you mean, full attention? And propping your book open? Why couldn't you just hold it like a normal human being?'

'Well, I was holding her.'

'You don't mean you pick her up every time she cries at night?'

'You don't mean you don't?'

We had a row, which it seemed like everyone in the family was with everyone else at the moment. I still had a cold. Dinner was miserable and I didn't sleep very well that night. My room was too hot and I kept dreaming I was trying to get somewhere across a city on a motorbike at night time but there kept being flights of steps in the way and things like that, or I would suddenly forget how to ride a motorbike.

Next day's exams were just as bad as French. I think I actually fell asleep in geography, and I didn't have time to finish the maths paper. What was even worse was what happened at lunch time.

I hadn't spoken to anyone all day because I'd nearly been late for registration, just nods and weak smiles at people in the morning. I was sitting on my own in the courtyard outside the lunch hall, looking at my maths book, and I saw Kiran. He walked past me; I only looked because he'd smiled at me, and then he stopped to have a word, obviously something funny, with Shantel Hardwick. I'd hardly ever actually seen her talking to anyone before; normally everyone around her chat-chats away and she just stares into space. In her massive high heels she was about three inches taller than Kiran, it looked stupid. I'd just turned back to my book when Lily Buckley came up and stood in front of me. I'd never known her very well, even though we'd been in the same class for years and years, but I'd always quite liked her, in fact I'd been a bit shocked that time in the park that it was her brother attacking Cal. I'd always thought she seemed like the kind of person I ought to be friends with.

She sat down very gracefully beside me, with her long legs and arms folding away all neat, and I sat up a bit and tried to straighten my shoulders. 'All right, Phoebe. How did you find the geography?'

'Rubbish,' I said, which I would have said anyway, of course. 'I'm terrible at geography.'

'You'd say that anyway.'

'Yeah, you're right. Geography is what I live for.'

She grinned. 'Me too, I just love it.'

'It's all those plate tectonics,' I said, looking down at my feet. There was a ladybird on the toe of my shoe.

'Listen,' she said, in front of everyone who was standing around, 'I wanted to apologise for Ryan. I heard all about it, he told me what he said. He's such a nasty little boy. I'm really sorry, it must have been horrible.'

'No,' I muttered, 'it's all right.'

'Calling you fat, that's not all right, Phoebe. You shouldn't have to put up with that stuff. I kicked him up and down. And teasing your little brother, I made him pay for it. Seriously, he won't do it again. He knows what my dad would say.'

'OK,' I said. My head was all hot. 'Well, thanks.' She went chirruping on again in a friendly way about the exams, but I could hardly see her I was so embarrassed. Luckily maths was about to start so I could say I had to go and get ready. I hate school sometimes. It isn't right when you're pleased to start a maths exam.

By now I was just chugging through the days, dying to go back to normal, though normal wasn't so normal really. The nights in my room, stuffy because the weather was, were feeling even longer than those first nights last week in the shed when Iris woke up all the time and my head hadn't learned yet how to go straight back to sleep as soon as she did.

Adam had a great big swollen face in the morning because he hadn't slept in so long. I thought it was absolutely amazing that Mum hadn't noticed it, but he said he'd hardly seen her because she was upstairs trying to wrestle Cal into his school uniform. Normally he'd have tried to help, but he knew I was waiting in the shed for him to come back so I could get off to school for more exams.

The only thing that happened that day other than trying to concentrate and not fall asleep on my face in the middle of an exam was that I saw Mr Rossy in the corridor at lunch time and suddenly was brave enough to go up to him.

'Mr Rossy,' I said, 'you know I auditioned for the play last week?'

'Yes,' he said, all impatient. 'The cast list will be up tomorrow, I've told everyone.'

'Yes, I know,' I said. 'I don't know if you'll have given me a part, but I don't think I can be in it, I'm afraid.'

'Oh?' His eyes got sharper. 'That's a shame. Let me just see...' He ruffled some pages.

'That's me,' I said, leaning over to point out my name and trying not to notice what was written opposite it. I didn't particularly want to know what part I would have got. It wasn't important at the moment.

'Right. Are you sure about this, er – Phoebe?'

'I am, thanks. I've just got too much else to do. Sorry,' I said.

'Right,' he said, and looked at me for a second, then bustled off again.

When I got home that evening I was feeling really downcast – not about the play, I didn't care about the play, but there was all this time I still had to spend revising and doing exams before they could be over. I'd even stopped at the baker's near the bus stop for a doughnut, which I hadn't done in ages because I'd had no money, and walked home stuffing it into my face and wiping the icing off with the back of my hand.

Dad was there when I got in, playing cards with Feng. He looked a bit pink and ruffled. 'How were the exams?'

'Fine,' I said, trying to be convincing because I didn't want to talk about it. 'Where's Cal?'

'He's upstairs,' Dad said grimly. 'He's not in a good way. I had to go and get him early because he pushed some little girl off the monkey bars this afternoon, and then he had to come with me to Feng's school to get him, so you can imagine how enjoyable that was.'

'She's not a little girl,' Feng said, putting down an ace. 'She's in my year and she's the same size as Mr Nicholls.' Mr Nicholls was the head teacher at Cal's school and he looked like a double-decker bus.

'It's particularly annoying because I was hoping to get Adam to babysit this evening, once he's home. I wanted to meet Mum at work and take her out for a drink. There're a few things we could do with talking about.'

'I bet.' I wasn't feeling especially sympathetic, but I put my school bag down. 'That'll be fine, Dad. You do it, we'll look after each other, right, Feng? Go now if you want, Adam'll be home any minute.'

'No, she doesn't even finish till half five, I've got plenty of time.'

'You could do with a shower,' Feng pointed out confidentially.

We got him to go by promising that I'd ring him if Adam wasn't home in ten minutes. Then I nipped up the garden to tell Adam. The curtains were drawn tight against the sunlight; Adam was bug-eyed and didn't even ask me about my exams. He said she hadn't slept all day. He said at this rate he'd have to spend the whole summer holiday in bed to recover. We talked about which of us was going to go and see to dinner, because Adam said he'd go insane if he had to look at the inside of the shed any more, but on the other hand he wasn't keen to make food or get involved with Cal. 'I'm telling you, I can't wait for your exams to be over. Though then I suppose it'll be all your stupid rehearsals every night.'

'No,' I said, 'I'm not doing the play anymore.'

''Course you are.'

'No, I'm not. I told Mr Rossy today...What?' He was looking at me suspiciously. 'It's not important enough, I haven't got time.' I didn't need to have it to think about. I had something else to do after all, which actually needed doing.

Before Adam could start telling me off for taking any excuse to be mediocre as usual we heard a pelting sound coming straight towards us. There was no time to do more than look at each other, terrified, before the door flew open with a *whang* that nearly shattered all the glass and Cal rolled in like a Tasmanian devil, arms and legs whirling, scattering all the things like nappies that were spread on the floor and kicking over the open tub of powdered milk so that it went flying and a cloud of it rose into the air. I breathed it in and it plastered the inside of my nose.

I'd been holding Iris, luckily, because he'd probably have landed on her if she'd been in her basket. As it was I'd got up and flown back against the wall with her clutched against me, and Adam had caught the swinging door before it went for another smash against more glass.

'CAL!' he bellowed. 'What are you DOING?'

Cal had stopped when he saw the bundle I was holding, and was open-mouthed though his fists were still clenched. 'What's that?'

'It's a baby,' I said in a cracked voice, because of the shock and the milk.

'What baby?'

'Cal, look what you've done! What's the matter with you?' Adam was shouting, partly because Iris had naturally started screaming after all the noise.

'Who is it?'

'She got left here,' I said testily, jiggling her up and down. 'We've been looking after her.'

'That's what you've been doing!' he said, his eyes lighting up. 'I knew something was going on.'

'Well, now you know. Stop walking in the milk.'

'Cal – look at this mess – you can't tell anyone. No one. Understand?' Adam was trying to save some of the milk and stare solemnly into Cal's eyes at the same time.

'Why?'

'Because if you tell, she'll be put into Care. And we

don't want that for her.' I feel bad saying things like that to Cal, even worse than to Feng because it feels like I'm criticising his life, and he's had it so tough I don't feel like I have any right to. But he nodded immediately, and came a bit closer. I had sat down to rock her and she was quiet again, looking up at me.

'No, 'course not. Unless she could stay here.' He put a hand out to touch her head. I remembered that Cal had a little sister, Lauren, who'd been left somewhere behind on his path of destruction, in one of the foster homes he'd been kicked out of.

Now that Iris had stopped screaming and the shed had stopped spinning I could hear Feng calling from somewhere, plaintively. I suppose Cal had just sprinted past him and he'd had no way to warn us. We left the shed for a bit and walked up the garden to let him know we were all right.

It was quite a relief, in some ways, being able to take her into the house even though it wasn't empty. I thought if only Mum and Dad would clear off for a while, we could manage nicely.

Chapter Ten

'All right,' Adam was saying as he served up the spaghetti, 'but really this is ridiculous. People keep finding out left right and centre. And, yeah, I trust you all to keep your mouths shut, and yes, Phoebe, maybe it's a good thing we've got a bit of help now, but it has to stop. We have to be more careful, because there's no one left now who can know about her. So you hear me, right, everyone?'

'Yes, boss,' I said, sprinkling grated cheese over my plate with one hand. The other was holding Iris's bottle; she was propped up in my lap on a cushion and the crook of my arm.

'It's not funny, Phoebe. Pass me that cheese.'

We were having an early dinner, with the back door open in case we needed to dive out, because we weren't sure what time Mum would be home, but it seemed a way of celebrating. Everyone was suddenly very cheerful, even

Adam. It was nice being able to have a chat with the baby around. Cal could hardly take his eyes off her and, along with the news that Dad was taking Mum out, the whole thing had completely shaken him out of his destructive mood. He even ate some of his tomatoes. Feng was delighted to have another look at Iris, since we hadn't been able to get him out to the shed since he'd found out about her. He held his finger over her face until she clutched at it. 'Look, she remembers me,' he said.

'Well, she hasn't met all that many people, Feng, why wouldn't she?'

'It's not that. We're friends, aren't we?' He bent over to kiss her and she swatted him in the face, trying to get hold of his glasses.

I found I wasn't caring about my exams again, and after all there were only two more days of them, although of course there would be the results all next week. But then I'd be skipping some days. I insisted to Adam that I was taking that night in the shed, I couldn't sleep in my room at the moment, anyway, and he agreed.

I supervised the washing up, which meant that Adam was the one holding her when we did hear Mum's key in the front door. He dashed out to the garden. Mum looked completely astonished when she found the rest of us in the kitchen doing the dishes and looking all peaceful with the radio on. 'Hello, what's going on? Who cooked dinner?'

'Adam did,' I said, taking off the rubber gloves. 'He's just gone to fetch something, I think. Did you have a nice time with Dad?'

'I did,' she said, pinching a bit of tomato out of the bowl. 'Don't get excited, it was just a drink. Where are you off to?'

'More revision,' I said, 'if that's OK. Now you're back I'll just zip out to the shed, it's where my books are...' I felt bad because she gave me a sympathetic, grateful look, as if she thought Adam and I had had to coordinate ourselves so as not to leave Feng and Cal alone in case Cal set fire to something, whereas the truth was it was Iris we couldn't leave alone.

Out in the shed Adam was looking much less giddy because he'd rediscovered the mess that we'd completely forgotten about. 'Don't worry about it,' I said, 'I'll clear it up once Iris is asleep.'

'Look, though, you left the tin of milk too near the door and I kicked the stupid thing over again. Now all the muslins and half her clothes are covered in powdered milk, as well as the rug...'

'You'll just have to do a big wash tomorrow.'

'Not the point. Look, the tin's practically empty.'

I saw there was barely enough at the bottom for a couple of bottles, if we scraped it. We'd had to shake out our school bags and all our pockets for pennies two days ago to buy the last lot of nappies, and there was nothing left. 'Do you think Feng or Cal might have a few quid kicking about?'

'No,' Adam said. 'Dad made Cal put everything he had in his moneybox towards the new DS, and Feng bought all that paper at the weekend, he needed the last lot of pocket money to have enough.' Feng liked drawing a lot, and he'd got oil pastels for his birthday which needed special paper. 'Don't you have anything left over?'

'No,' I said, and sat down with a flump. It was all too hard again. 'I bought a doughnut on the way home and that was my last forty pence.'

'Funny. I bought a doughnut this morning with my last forty pence.'

'How did you do that?' I asked suspiciously.

'I took her out in the pushchair,' he confessed.

'Adam! What if someone had seen you?'

'I thought about it and decided that no one could who would possibly know that Mum and Dad hadn't fostered a baby recently.'

'But what if the guy in the baker's shop says to Mum next time she's in, "Nice baby, shame about your eldest son"?'

'I know. Sorry. I've just been going so mad stuck in here all week. I think I'm losing it. And I can't lose it, I know, because—'

I didn't want to think about that any more than he did, and Adam had to go because otherwise Mum might have come looking for him, so I told him not to worry. 'We'll do what we need to. We just have to decide what that is.' We both said we'd think about it and talk in the morning – there was just enough milk to get us through the night.

I did start racking my brains the moment Adam left, all the time I was tidying up the shed, making a big pile of powdery clothes and the ones Cal had stepped all over with his dirty trainers, and then giving Iris a bath and feeding her. I didn't come up with anything till the middle of the night, when I was so tired I realised that there was one obvious solution.

In the morning, it turned out that Adam had decided on the same thing. I suppose in a different sort of family we might have got away with begging the money off Mum, but none of us could ask Mum for ten pounds without explaining exactly what it was for, and we couldn't think of anything that she would believe and wouldn't find out about afterwards. We couldn't steal it from her, either, for the same reason – not because she would have been furious, though she really would have been, but because there wouldn't be any way of explaining it away afterwards. If we ever did a thing like that she'd watch us like some kind of prison guard for months after. She might easily not have any cash on her, anyway, she often didn't.

Which really left getting the milk without paying for it, which meant stealing it from a shop. Of course I was worried about the idea of getting caught; I'd never shoplifted in my life before, and if Adam had he wasn't admitting it to me. I knew a lot of people who had though. Some girls in my class do it all the time, at lunch breaks and after school. So I knew it was possible to get away with it. I just didn't know if it would be possible for me. Adam said it had to be me, because if anyone saw him, or any boy his age, lingering near the baby stuff they'd start following him straight away because they'd know he had to be up to no good. I didn't think I was really a very obvious person to be looking at powdered milk either, but he was right, it was better for me to do it. I think he'd much rather have done it himself, because he didn't trust me not to get caught and if I was, obviously that would be the end of everything. Also, he doesn't like not being in charge.

Probably the best place to try would have been a huge supermarket just because there are so many more people there, but it was already half past six when we were sitting having this conversation; I had to be at school for a history exam at nine o'clock that morning and I had to get the milk first, and all the big shops are well out of the way.

Cal, who was sitting in his Batman pyjamas with us because, Adam said, he had insisted on climbing down the tree and coming to the shed too, offered to come to the corner shop down the road with me and cause a distraction. I could see just what he had in mind, but we decided that a six-year-old causing a ruckus at that time of the morning would just make more people look at me as the person he was with. So instead I went in as usual, got ready for school, told Mum I had to be there really early to go over some revision with some of my friends, went back to the shed and changed out of my uniform – just in case I was chased – and went up the road to the shops.

It would have been easier to steal from the chemist's, because it's quite big and dark and the people who run it are always behind the counter, but it had only just opened for the morning and there might not have been any other customers in there, and anyway if I did get caught they would probably recognise me and remember who my parents were. So I went to the corner shop, which is really a very small supermarket. There are signs up there saying that they have security, cameras and stuff, and it's true, the cameras are there, but the girls at school always say they don't really work, and I did think that a shop that size would be unlikely to have anyone sitting in a back room just watching cameras all day.

What made it difficult was that I didn't have enough money to buy something else from the shelf the milk was on; it was with all the nappies and the toiletries and stuff, and quite near things like washing-up liquid, and you couldn't get any of that for fifty-three pence which was all the four of us had managed to scrape together. So I had no excuse to linger. But you could see that shelf from the sweets display, so I hung around pretending to look at chocolate bars – I was actually looking at them a bit because you can't get many of those for fifty-three pence either – picked one up, then wandered round the corner. I was holding my jacket flopped over my arm and as I went past the milk shelf I scooped a tin off the corner with my forearm so it was under the jacket. I didn't dare to stop and check it was completely hidden, so when I got to the counter I was terrified. My heart was pounding in my ears.

There was only one person ahead of me. When it was my turn I sort of dipped down so the jacket was hanging more forward, put the bar down, gave him the change which was all sweaty from my hand, then half turned away while he was counting it. That's when I saw that the cameras did work – there were four tiny little TV screens arranged in a square right in front of him, showing all the corners of the shop, including the one I'd just been in. I must have walked past those screens hundreds of times without ever noticing them. I nearly dropped the tin on the floor; I was still expecting him to say, at best, 'And that tin you're holding costs ten pounds ninety-five,' but all he actually said as he slammed his till drawer shut was, 'Thank you.' I only just remembered to pick up the chocolate bar before I ran out.

Adam was on the corner holding my uniform in a bag. We'd had to risk leaving Iris alone for ten minutes, just like I had to risk Mum cycling past, or Dad driving by with Cal and Feng and seeing me in my ordinary clothes, still here when I ought to be well on my way to school. I passed him the milk. It was the wrong brand, because our usual one had been on the middle of the shelf and I couldn't have slipped it off so easily. Then I had to run. I really hate running.

After I got to school and managed to slip in and get changed in the toilets without any of the teachers having noticed I had my own clothes on, I calmed down a bit. I felt great then. Everyone around me was all pale and nervous about the exam, and I'm sure I had a great big smile on my face. That was easily my best paper. I was the most awake I had been that week, for one thing. I even chatted to some people afterwards at lunch. I had been avoiding them all. All I'd really wanted to do at lunch and break times was sit in the library or the classroom with a book open and sort of go to sleep with my eyes open. In a way I was lucky it had been exam time, because there had been a lot of people doing the same thing.

Charlotte said she hadn't seen me all week.

'Yeah, you have. You were crying all over me on Monday.'

'Well, that's ages ago. Hey, guess what, my dad promised to buy me a TV if I've done well. For my room, you know.'

'Cool.'

'So my mum got crazy angry with him because she's a fascist about TV, you know.'

'And have you done well, do you reckon?'

'No, I've cocked every single one up. But it's OK because Mum will make Dad buy it for me anyway in the end.'

I felt very fond of her, even though it was difficult for me to care right then, or even pretend to care, about the things we all normally talk about at school.

After the second exam I went home with other people too; it was the first time for about two weeks I hadn't just run off on my own after school. It all felt a bit silly but it was quite nice and comforting, to hear them talking about TV programmes and each other and how badly all the exams had gone and how wonderful it would be when they were over.

When I got home Mum met me at the front door and said she was just dashing up the road to buy a packet of classy biscuits because Stephen the social worker was coming round.

I was surprised because normally we know in advance but I think Mum had known for a while and she was springing it on us on purpose because she didn't want us to worry. It hadn't worked; when I went in Cal and Feng were all in a tizzy because suddenly, this time, they could see the point in saying exactly the right things and making Mum out to be a fantastic foster carer. Although Cal always got anxious around Stephen – like he did around most people – before it was always about himself and what he thought might happen to him.

I got into a bit of a flap too, and because we didn't have much time for running about I called Adam from the house phone – it had been ages since we had any spare cash to put credit on our mobiles, but we kept them switched on for emergencies like this. Anyway, I knew Mum would want him to be here if Stephen was coming round.

'All right,' he was saying as he came in through the back door, 'now don't panic, anyone. No reason there should be a problem. The main thing is to keep Stephen out of the garden.'

'Why would he go in the garden?' I asked.

'Well, exactly. Though it would be safer if he wasn't in the kitchen either, in case Iris cries. She probably will, being on her own. So we'd better have Mum in the front room too. Phoebe, you'll make the tea when he gets here.' Adam was loving being boss. 'You two, we'll have to keep him occupied.'

'It's them he'll want to talk to,' I pointed out. 'He could talk to Mum anytime on the phone if he wanted.'

'Right. So, nice and normal, yes?'

'You'll have to make an effort, Cal,' Feng said, fixing him with his big shiny brown eyes. 'It's our job to prove this is a good place to live, that it makes us be good, OK? Even now when it's just Gillian?' Cal nodded, all solemn. Adam grinned at me over their heads.

Stephen is pretty nice actually. He's the first man we've had, and I suppose he's on the young side, younger than Mum and Dad, anyway. He arrived just after Mum got back and as she was making a fan of chocolate biscuits on a white plate; he was looking a bit tense but I got him and Mum to sit down and said I'd make the tea. I'd already arranged Feng on the sofa, and Stephen sat beside him. Then, when I was standing in the kitchen doorway asking him about milk and sugar, Cal came down the stairs, all sedate, with his hair combed. I would have advised against that if he'd asked me, it looked too different, but he was obviously very happy with himself and sat down on Stephen's other side. I could see Adam trying not to laugh, and Mum too, though she didn't know what was happening.

'Hello, Stephen,' Cal said, when he had sat right back

on the sofa. His feet didn't come much past the edge of the seat.

'Hello, Cal,' Stephen said, equally polite, not looking at any of us. 'How are you?'

'I'm fine, thank you.'

'How are you, Stephen?' Feng asked.

'Yes, how are you?' echoed Cal.

Stephen's head turned between them. 'I'm very well, thank you, boys.'

'Oh good,' Feng beamed.

'So we're all well,' Cal said happily.

'Er...' Stephen flashed a glance at the rest of us. I blatantly hadn't gone to make the tea, because I was too busy watching. I ducked into the kitchen, but didn't put the kettle back on yet because I wanted to listen.

'I'm actually here just for a bit of a catch-up,' Stephen was saying, 'a bit of a chat, really, about school and home and all that.'

'Home is great,' Cal said. 'School is terrible,' he added, sounding murderous for a second, 'but home is great.'

'Right.'

'How's that tea coming, Phoebe?' Adam called, and I switched the kettle back on guiltily.

As I brought in the tray that Mum had already set, Stephen was saying, 'So I thought we could chat about some of the changes you've all been going through lately.'

Adam stood up, 'I guess you don't need me then, so I'll be upstairs.'

'No,' Stephen said mildly, and we stopped backing away, 'if you don't mind, Adam, Phoebe, I'd love to hear what's been happening with you too.'

It was like swimming in custard trying to talk sensibly and correctly about Dad being gone; even more than it might usually have been because all of us had our eyes on the clock, even Cal who can't tell the time yet. We'd never left Iris alone this long before, and she hadn't even been asleep. Our eyes were getting bigger and bigger.

'Well,' Adam was saying, 'yes, of course it's difficult. I don't know, I mean, I suppose we're all still hoping he might come back. What do you think, Phoebe?'

'Yes, I think that's right,' I said mechanically.

'Things are still a bit unsettled,' Mum said. She looked upset. I suppose we hadn't really had this conversation yet just on our own, without any social workers.

'It's all right, Gillian,' Cal said loudly. 'I don't mind. I like it better now actually.'

'Do you, Cal?' Stephen asked, rearranging his legs and sipping his tea. 'Why's that?'

Cal looked at the rest of us as if he suddenly realised he was on dangerous ground. 'Because I like Gillian so much.'

'And we still see a lot of my dad,' Adam put in. 'He

163

comes round all the time.'

'All the time,' I agreed. 'Helps us with our homework and stuff, doesn't he, Feng?'

'Phoebe's actually helping Feng with his reading,' Mum told Stephen. 'His teacher says he's making great progress.'

'Is that right? Well done, both of you. Do you enjoy that, Feng?'

'I need to go to the toilet,' Feng said. Stephen immediately got up to offer to take him and then stood politely out of the way; as he and Mum were stepping around each other Feng lurched himself up on the back of the sofa and knocked Cal's half-sucked biscuit out of his hand so that it slid in a blur of wet chocolate down the sofa front and stuck halfway. Feng was a genius. We should have had him in on it from the start.

Our sofa is sort of blonde – we inherited it from one of Mum's friends who changes her furniture all the time – so someone had to run for a cloth. Adam and I clashed trying to get through the kitchen doorway. 'I'll go,' he hissed and went out the back door. Cal had caught on straight away and was making a total meal of the situation. 'My biscui-i-i-i-i-it,' he was wailing, his face all screwed up.

'Sorry, Cal,' Feng said from the other doorway; Stephen was carrying him up to the bathroom.

'You can have another one, Cal,' Mum shouted. 'It's *fine.*'

'I want *that* one.' Getting a bit carried away, he pulled one of the back cushions off the sofa and threw it at the table where the tea tray was.

'Perhaps this isn't the best time, Gillian,' Stephen said, after he'd brought Feng back downstairs and Mum had managed to get Cal up to his bedroom to calm down.

'I'm sorry,' she said, sounding exhausted. 'I thought he was doing really well till that happened, not sure where it came from today.'

'It was my fault,' Feng said serenely.

'He's actually been much better, just lately,' I said, looking up from the floor where I was still picking up bits of mug. 'Hasn't he, Mum?'

'I suppose he has,' she said, sounding a bit doubtful. 'For the last couple of days.'

'I think he found you coming round a bit stressful,' I told Stephen. 'Wouldn't you say, Feng? He's been a bit worried that, with Dad leaving, he might get moved on as well.'

Mum looked at me sharply, but Stephen, sounding interested, said, 'I suppose that's a natural step for him to take. He talks to you, does he, Phoebe?'

'Sometimes,' I said, trying to sound as if I would be reluctant to betray any confidences.

'A little bit of reassurance, then,' he said, looking at Mum, who nodded. 'And I must try to get him to stop seeing me as the harbinger of doom.'

'Oh,' Feng said kindly, 'that's how he sees everyone outside the family.'

Chapter Eleven

After we got everything sorted out and Cal had trailed downstairs and said sorry, it ended up being a good evening. Mum was all jolly and full of reading stories to the little boys and putting sprinkles on the ice cream without us even asking. Feng got the giggles all the time when he was overexcited, and Cal would actually touch you without hurting you. Even Adam was in a better mood and said he was ready for another night in the shed, though he warned me I could take on the whole weekend because he'd had enough of it and needed to get out and get some exercise or something.

Friday was great in school as well because of exams finishing, and there were lots of shrieks and shouts when the day was over. I had to go straight home though because Mum and Dad were going to a concert at Feng's school and Adam was meant to be going round to his friend's house, so I had to babysit Cal for a couple of hours. I didn't mind. He was so rarely in a good mood like he'd been lately that right now looking after him was like a holiday.

Adam was sort of half keen to get out of the shed and half not very about going to see his friend Lucas. 'I won't be back till late. You'll have to think of some excuse to be out here all evening. Why don't you say—'

'We'll be fine, Adam. Go,' I said.

Cal came out to the shed with two Kit Kats after Adam had left and we sat and ate them and looked at Iris. It had been a hot grey day, but since I left school the haziness had rolled back and the sky was bright deep blue. I got us all sitting on the grass but Cal had ants in his pants after a day at school, a week without much running time, I suppose. We would have to tell Mum we didn't mind Cal playing in the garden now, but we couldn't do it yet because then it would seem weird if we made a fuss whenever she stepped out of the back door. Anyway, he'd boiled up too much now for even the garden and after bouncing off the hedges a bit he said he wanted to go to the park.

'But we can't go to the park.'

'I want an ice cream,' he said. Mum had left me some money for ice creams in case I took him out but I'd sort of assumed we would keep it for the next lot of milk or nappies we needed. I'd forgotten Cal was only six. Actually,

I wanted an ice cream too. I looked from Cal to Iris to the tartan pushchair, half hidden behind the open shed door.

Adam would have killed me, even though he'd taken her out to get a doughnut just a few days ago. But at least that had been during the day when it would have been really bad luck to bump into anyone we knew.

We'd no sooner got near the park than it dawned on me that people look at children pushing prams. No one spoke to us and no one gave us dirty looks exactly, I think it was more that I noticed when they noticed. Maybe they even thought it was sweet. Or maybe it was Iris; she was definitely looking more like the kind of baby people want to coo over. When she was asleep it was like a Christmas card. Cal started glaring back at people and I had to tell him not to.

I didn't want to go near the playground, not after last time; if someone rang Mum up just to tell her that Cal had got into a scrap she'd be bound to hear that we'd been seen there with a new baby in a pushchair. We went to the duck pond instead. I'd brought some bread. Cal ran round and round for a while and then I bought two ice creams and we sat on a bench and fed the ducks. I would have liked to get Iris out and squat down with her to look at the coots but I didn't dare in case it got more people looking at us. There was a family of ducklings swimming around in the middle of the pond, half-grown but still fluffy – their mother was showing lots of sense to keep them well away from the edges where Cal had been belting about.

Cal scoffed all his ice cream in about twenty seconds and I ended up giving him the end of mine because I couldn't hold it and push the pushchair, and I wanted to move away from the pond. There were other people around now and I thought they might recognise us. With having brothers at different schools I don't know who Mum knows and who she doesn't.

We were walking up the path towards the tennis courts, having an argument about what to watch when we got back, when someone said my name. I hadn't even noticed anyone near us, but Kiran was standing right there. He was wearing a blue T-shirt and these cropped trousers and swinging a tennis racquet around. 'Hi,' he said. 'Been having an ice cream?'

'Yes,' I said, looking from hand to hand and then realising I must have smudges on my face. I clawed at it. 'Been playing tennis?' I asked stupidly.

'I feel like I've been cooped up in a hot room revising for ten years,' he said, stretching up with both arms behind his head and his racquet down his back, and then yawning so that the tip of his tongue came out above his bottom teeth. 'Glad they're over?'

'So glad,' I said, looking down at Cal and seeing that he was in a panic, which had come out as him absolutely glowering at Kiran. Kiran noticed it at the same time and stopped yawning. 'This is my little brother, Cal,' I told him. 'And you've met Iris.' I poked Cal in the back as hard as I could to let him know I was in control of the situation. I was glad I'd told Kiran he was a bit weird.

He wandered along beside us for a bit, chatting. He got nothing out of Cal but I did my best to be funny and at ease and he stayed with us. I couldn't decide whether I needed to keep Cal with me or if I should send him off to the playground, but I left it because I couldn't be sure he'd go. He was keeping a very close watch on Kiran.

So there we were, and we'd skirted the courts and were just coming up to the gate that leads back out of the park towards our street. I was looking up at Kiran and so was Cal, and so neither of us noticed who was coming round the corner, at least not till it was far too late to run.

'Hello,' said Mum. She was all surprised and interested and Mum-like. I hadn't seen her eyes light up like that for ages.

'Mum!' I said, and dried up.

Kiran shifted his racquet to under his other arm and leaped forward to shake her hand. 'Hi there, I'm Kiran. I've seen you around with Phoebe, I think.'

Mum went all fluttery. 'Hello, I'm Gillian. Very pleased to meet you. Did you just happen to bump into Phoebe, then?'

'That's right.'

'We go to the same school,' I interrupted.

'Of course. Well, and who's this?' She was looking tenderly into the pushchair.

Kiran was still wearing his glowing adult-impressing expression. He smiled into midair as Mum bent down to look at the baby, then it suddenly dawned on him and he looked at me. I was staring at him in complete terror. Cal was clutching the pushchair handle like he was drowning, and looking up at Kiran too with his mouth open.

'Oh,' said Kiran, 'sorry. This is my cous— er, niece. Iris.'

'She's lovely,' Mum said. 'Aren't you beautiful? How old is she?'

'Four weeks,' I said quickly. 'She's nice, isn't she? Kiran let us push her.'

'Brave of you to let Cal near her,' Mum said, straightening up. 'Now, Cal, I was joking. I'm sorry to interrupt your walk, toodles, but I need you to come home. I've sent your dad and Feng out for fish and chips and they'll be back before us if we don't hurry up.'

There was just nothing to be done, or if there was I couldn't think of it. I said a completely agonised goodbye to Kiran; I hardly dared look at him but as far as I could tell he was poker-faced. Cal was more reluctant than I was, I had to drag his hands off the pushchair handle, and all without Mum noticing. I couldn't even say bye to Iris, and anyway I didn't want to scare her. I had to walk off, holding Cal round the wrist and stiff-arm dragging him along, without even looking back.

There was no way of telling Feng what had happened, but he knew something had even before he saw us because Mum had gone springing into the garden to call us when they all got back from the concert – it was just as well I'd remembered to lock the shed or she'd have seen all the baby stuff. Feng had had to chat to Dad all the way to the chip shop and back whilst worrying that Mum would bump straight into us, exactly like she did. And then Dad wheeled him back in and we were both sitting at the table with empty plates in front of us, and no sign of the baby. We all had to choke down dinner looking at each other with round eyes and stiff faces, because we weren't on our own for a second. I was sort of aware that Mum and Dad seemed to be getting on better than they had in ages, but I couldn't concentrate enough to be pleased.

Then, as we were finishing and I was trying to think of a way to get us all out to the shed, Adam walked into the kitchen. He'd come back early from his friend's house because he smelled fish and chips, he said, all cheerful, and was rooting round in the papers for the chips that were left over when he did a sudden double take and I saw him count us and realise something was wrong. 'Er,' he said. 'Er, Phoebe, I need to talk to you about something. Have you finished? Will you come out to the shed a sec?'

Sometimes it was best to stick as close to the truth as you could and hope it was so close no one would look further. 'OK,' I said, 'I was just thinking the same thing. But I think Cal and Feng should come too.'

Dad laughed, especially as we all ground our chairs back at the same time and Cal jumped to the door. 'Is this you lot avoiding the washing up?'

'Definitely,' I said, opening the door for Cal. Adam picked Feng up to bring him out. We'd have to think of some all-child surprise for Mum later or something, but at least right now we were outside on our own.

Cal and I galloped down the garden to the corner as quick as we could. Adam was coming behind us, wheezing from carrying Feng; I'd heard Dad offer to help, but Adam carried Feng around the house all the time. The only reason he was breathing hard now was that he was running, with his knees bent weirdly. I went and unlocked the shed door and opened it, as if some miracle might have happened and she'd be in there in her basket, then sat down on the step. I was ready to cry from nerves and panic. It was an hour already since I'd left Iris in the park. It would be getting dark soon and I had no idea where she was. It was time for her bottle.

Adam didn't say anything at first when we told him

what had happened. I didn't dress it up because there was no point. Neither of us could say what we were thinking because the kids were already white and Feng's eyes were full of water. I'd been telling myself it would be fine since we turned out of the park gate and now I tried telling them. 'I know we don't know him well but we know who he *is*. He goes to my school, he even lives round here.'

'But you don't know where,' Cal pointed out.

'Not exactly, but it's somewhere close by. In fact completely close by, it's just over that wall. And he knows where we live, so . . .'

'So what?'

'So I suppose he'll just bring her back,' I said lamely.

Adam pulled up some grass. 'Do you think I should try and climb over the wall and see if he's there?'

'No,' I said. 'Because if you get caught by his parents that's it, you'd have to explain.'

'And explain that we not only had her, but we lost her as well,' he agreed.

I got up and went to put the kettle on. If she did come back she'd need her bottle. 'I lost her. But, look, she's safe. He's not going to run off with her.'

'How do you know?' Cal demanded.

'What if he just leaves her somewhere?' Feng asked.

We sat in silence, all looking at the ground, for a moment. Under the trees the light was getting dim. Mum would come looking for the boys soon. Mind you, now there was no Iris all we would have to do is pull the shed door shut again so she didn't see the nappies and baby clothes and mess.

Adam jumped up. 'Come on, Phoebe. He might still be in the park. If he'd taken her home we'd probably know about it by now. Quick.'

But just then there was a sudden scraping on the other side of the wall, behind Adam's head, and a whistle. It confused us because it didn't come from Kiran's garden but from the alleyway at the side of ours. Then Kiran's voice called, low like a birdwatcher, 'Phoebe!'

We'd put a few bricks against the wall to act as a step if we needed to go out or come in that way again, though in the mornings I always tried to slip out through the house. Adam was up straddling the wall in a second. I only managed to get my stomach up and balance across it, looking down at Kiran. It was gloomy in the alleyway but I could see his teeth again, and the pale blue of Iris's blanket.

'Oh! Christ,' I said, at the same time as Adam said, 'Where have you been?'

Kiran sounded a bit sharp, 'Around and about. As you were coming back for dinner I thought I'd better give you a while. Here.' He bent down and took the blanket off Iris, then tossed it up to Adam, who caught it.

I slid back down the wall, scraping my stomach so it was quite sore, and said to Cal and Feng, 'It's all right, he's got her.'

Adam leaned down and when he straightened up again he had Iris in his arms. She was complaining and he passed her down to me. She felt like the best thing in the world. I was nearly sick with relief and plunked down with her, crooning, next to Feng, Cal crowding up behind. Adam was fumbling with something; it was the pushchair, folded. He dropped it onto the grass and jumped down himself. Next thing Kiran was over the wall in our garden too.

'Come on over,' Adam said coldly.

Kiran looked at him, then spoke to me. 'What the *hell* is going on? What are you lot doing with a baby your mother knows nothing about?'

'I'm not sure you really want to know that, do you?' Adam asked. He had folded his arms and was leaning on the wall. He wasn't as tall as Kiran but maybe I'd been wrong to think that Kiran looked much older.

'Look,' Kiran said, 'when I get stuck with a baby I don't know but who I've just said is my niece, and I don't have a clue what to do with her, that makes it my business who she is and what I'm bringing her back to, OK?'

I told him the story. Even Adam must have seen that we had to. And Kiran stopped talking like an adult and in a raised voice and just looked worried. I recognised the look, I'd been seeing nothing else lately. 'I still don't see how you think you can keep her.'

'Well, we have done so far,' I said. I'd made up a bottle and it was nearly cool enough to give her. She was being very good.

'Yes, for a while, and it looks like it's nearly killed you,' he said, looking round at all of us. 'But you can't believe you'll be able to do it for much longer.'

'We'll do it as long as we can,' Adam said, 'because of the alternative.'

'You mean, her being taken away?'

'Because of what would happen to her,' Adam explained. 'You haven't met Leanne.'

'But she doesn't want the baby.'

'She said she didn't, but if Social Services gets involved they'll be dragging her in and she might decide she may as well have Iris as have all the trouble over her, and that would be terrible because she's in a bad situation herself and she's not a good person, either.'

'Lots of people aren't good people and they make fine parents,' said Kiran.

'Who says?'

'I do. It's to make up for the fact that lots of OK people turn out to be terrible at it,' he said. It sounded like he knew what he was talking about. You never know about people, and what they might have seen.

'Maybe all that's true, but believe me, Kiran.' It was the first time Adam had used his name. 'You don't know Leanne. She's just one of those people who makes a giant mess of everything they touch. She's not someone you'd want in your life and I don't want her near this baby. She knew it herself, that's why she brought her here. And . . .' He hesitated. 'When I say the situation was bad, we don't know exactly what it was. But Leanne had bruises on her face.'

'So shouldn't you tell someone even more then, so this Leanne can get some help?' Kiran said.

I'd worried about that too sometimes, but Adam was firm on it. 'She's not our responsibility. She's an adult. And her concern was for Iris. It was Iris that she wanted to be here, so she could be safe and not in Care.'

'OK, well, say I take your word for it.' He was sitting cross-legged between Feng and Cal and opposite me. 'What do you think is going to happen? I mean, seriously? You're not planning to keep her in this shed till she's old enough to leave home, are you?'

'No,' I said. 'We don't know what's going to happen. We're just trying to keep her safe as long as we can.'

'Aren't you afraid of what might happen when they do find out?' His eyes flicked delicately from one side to the other. Of course I knew what he meant. Of course when I woke up at night in a certain mood with the owls hooting outside I thought about whether we were risking losing not only Iris but also Feng and Cal, if Social Services thought Mum and Dad should have been keeping a better eye on us.

'Look,' Adam said, 'I know we can't answer all your questions. And you could shop us properly if you felt like it. But we hope you won't.'

'Yes,' I said, 'we hope that.'

'Because this is what we're doing, and we've got our reasons.'

'I can see that,' Kiran said.

'And we're looking after her properly. She's fed well and she's clean and she's happy.'

'Oh!' I had looked down to check if Iris was awake and caught something I hadn't seen before, ever. 'Adam, look! Look!' She was smiling, up at me; her face was lit by the rays of the setting sun which reached over the wall, those broad flat rays you can see and that turn everything they touch pale gold. I forgot everything else. She was looking right at me.

There was a scuffle to see and I'm not sure if anyone did but me and Feng, who happened to be closest and on the right side, but after a minute everyone sat down again as if they had.

'She's not supposed to do that yet,' said Adam.

'Maybe she's older than you thought,' Kiran suggested.

'Or maybe she's just super-advanced,' I said.

'Either way, you couldn't really ask for a better sign.' Kiran jumped to his feet and stretched. 'Settles the question, really.'

Adam looked up at him. 'So you're not going to grass us up?'

'I wouldn't have done. I believed you even without the sentimental touch.'

'Right,' Adam said. 'Well, good. It's time to go in, Mum'll be getting suspicious. If you stay here, Phoebe, I'll carry Feng in, and then come back and you can go in and do the evening bit. Time for you to go too, mate.'

'I know,' Kiran said, putting his foot against the back wall. The tree bent low enough for him to reach up to it. 'I do have parents of my own, you know.'

Chapter Twelve

That was a crazy-feeling evening, and Saturday too. It was a relief to have the exams over, but of course a much greater one to get Iris back, and for Kiran to say he wouldn't tell anyone. Everyone was happy. And it didn't make me less happy that I'd sort of had a moment when I knew, really knew I mean, what it would be like if Iris was gone. I think Adam probably felt the same, though we didn't talk about it. It was like underneath everything there was this great big feeling, worry and peace at the same time, and it didn't seem to affect what was going on on top much. It didn't stop me getting annoyed with Adam, for instance, or with Cal when he busted into my room in the middle of my nap on Saturday morning; and it didn't make it less embarrassing when I was helping Mum put the shopping away and she started talking about Kiran.

'So, he goes to your school, does he?'

'Mmm.'

'You've never mentioned him.'

'I don't know him that well.'

'How come he's got a white niece?'

'I don't know,' I said carelessly, 'maybe her mother's his half-sister, or something. Don't know.'

'What year is he in?'

'Same as Adam. He was the one who came first in the entrance exam, remember, to Adam's school.'

'Of course! Of course. I remember now, he left, didn't he? So...he's at yours now. That's interesting.' She was trying to fit a bag of plain flour into the high cupboard where all the baking stuff is – we can't keep it lower or Cal gets into the sugar. 'I thought he seemed...' She turned round and leaned her elbows on the table, where I was filling the fruit bowl. 'I'm searching for the *mot juste*, but all I can come up with is gorgeous.'

'Mum!' I wailed.

'Sorry,' she said, ruffling my hair. 'I just wondered if that's why you've seemed so different lately.'

'I haven't seemed different,' I muttered, biting through the orange bag.

'Up in that shed all the time, dreamy. Getting on with your brothers – all of them. And you look different too.'

'How?'

She peered into my face. 'Mostly tired. But there is

something else as well.' She drifted away to see what Cal was doing.

Kiran kept appearing. I guess he did have parents but he must have had them well in order. When I went down to the shed after lunch – Adam had been there all morning, trying to catch up on schoolwork he'd picked up from Lucas the day before – Kiran had just arrived and was lying on his back in the sun. Iris was on a blanket next to him. I went to turn her onto her tummy for a minute, because the book said you were meant to so they got used to it and would learn to crawl. Cal was with me too; last night, Adam and I had pinched fifteen minutes before I nipped back out of his window, installed Cal as a babysitter – he was quite handy at climbing down the tree – and had a casual conversation with Mum where we mentioned that we thought it would be good for Cal and Feng, when there was someone to carry him, to be allowed access to the shed. Particularly as a trust thing, because it was an adult-free zone. She had been a bit cautious, but pleased with us.

Since we were all there, Adam went to get Feng. When he came back he said Mum was in shock over having time to herself, and had gone off into town saying she was going round her lover's house. We took this as more disgusting but valuable evidence that she was feeling better. I wondered what Dad was doing.

I turned Iris back round because she didn't like her front much; she couldn't really lift her head up; and she fell asleep. I think we'd tired her out because all of us had been trying to get her to smile whenever we got near her. Feng settled down to draw her, and Kiran brought our old swing ball pole out from behind the shed and set it up, a safe distance away, for Cal. It was a lovely day; the shade from the trees kept it from being too hot but it was warm enough to be sleepy, and so still you could hear bees buzzing in all the roses.

'Phoebe,' Feng said to me, still studying Iris and then his paper. 'What you and Adam said to Kiran last night about Leanne.'

'What about it?' I asked. Adam looked up watchfully.

'I mean, about the reason we're hiding Iris, because we don't want Leanne to have to come back.'

'Yes,' Adam said.

'That's not what you told me the reason was.' He looked up at Adam with his clear brown eyes.

'There are heaps of reasons to keep her like we are, Feng,' I said.

'And they're all good reasons,' Adam said, in his most end-of-conversation voice. We avoided looking at each other. They were all good reasons. And half our audience

185

was strictly PG. We had had to pick the right argument to convince each person, that was all.

Cal came back with a sweaty T-shirt and flopped down beside Feng. 'That's a good drawing.'

'It is, actually, Feng,' I said, looking at it upside-down.

'You'll have to tear it up, though,' Adam said. I protested, but he said, 'What if Mum sees it?'

'He can keep it well hidden,' I said.

'We ought to keep it,' Cal piped up, his freckled face serious. 'We ought to be taking lots of photos, really.'

'Oh, yes?' Adam said.

'Yes. Look how many baby pictures there are of you both. It's what people do with babies.'

Adam and I didn't say anything because it was true. Kiran dropped down on the grass opposite us. His clothes were unmarked, but then he'd just been standing there swatting idly while Cal raced around missing the ball, or else hitting it so hard it flew up in the air and made the string all loose. 'You can borrow my camera if you're afraid of someone seeing them.'

'What if your parents find them?'

'I'll just put them on a memory stick and delete them from the camera straight away,' he said. 'No problem.'

'Oooh, yes!' I said, before Adam could pick more holes. 'Let's do it. Come on, Adam, we really should. It is what people do. And Iris should have some baby pictures of herself, you know, for when she's older.' Wherever she was then.

Kiran nipped over the fence – he could practically just swing over it by now, it must have been like our tree, you just had to get used to it and you forgot it was there – and was back in ten minutes with a little camera. It was red and looked flashier than ours. He took a ton of photos.

'You've got enough to need two memory sticks,' Adam complained after a while.

'I'm not a photographer. I've got to take a lot if you want any decent ones,' Kiran said, looking up. 'Cal, straighten your face. You look like a ginger monkey.'

Adam had the baby that night, and he was less cheerful when I wandered in yawning early in the morning, with wet feet from the dew. 'I think she might have a cold coming on. She was snuffling all night.'

'Oh,' I said, dismayed. 'Maybe we should have kept a blanket on her yesterday. She was in the shade all the time.'

He snorted. 'It was red-hot yesterday. She's just caught that cold we all had last week. Or maybe it's Kiran, bringing in new germs. Whatever. She slept all right, really, but when she did wake up she screamed, and

I thought she might . . .' He hesitated. 'I thought she might be a bit hot.'

There wasn't much we could do about it then, but we weren't happy about the idea of her getting sick. It was going to be another hot day and the books said to keep her cool, so I brought down the electric fan I usually got dibs on for my room in the summer. There wasn't much else we could do, besides put her in just a vest. We didn't have any hot-weather clothes, really, and I didn't want to put nothing on her, not when she was ill, it felt wrong.

It was Sunday, but we couldn't go swimming because there was a swimathon at the pool, so Dad came over before lunch and took us to the Natural History Museum. Cal was in an outrageous sulk because of the swimming. He normally likes the museum; they have stuffed animals there you can stroke, and he runs up and down the marbled aisles while everyone winces and waits for him to crash into a glass case, but he was edgy and he got into a scrap with another boy at the drawing table over the red felt tip and hit him in the face, so Dad said he had to leave. Feng hadn't finished his drawing yet and Dad had promised to take him to see the shrunken heads, so I had to get Cal out and leave them to it. Dad gave me some money to buy us each an ice lolly, because he's a softy.

There was an ice-cream van parked just outside the museum, but we went through the big car park and up the street to a newsagent for the lollies instead. That saved nearly two pounds, which on top of it being pocket-money day meant we should be all right for milk and nappies that week. It was baking hot on the street, but we couldn't go back into the museum lobby with lollies, so we loitered as close as we could to a shop with an awning, to get the shade. I tried to stop Cal wiping his hands all over the shop window, but he was distracted by looking in.

'Look,' he said, with sticky orange dripping from his mouth. 'That's a nice dress.' It happened to be a shop that sold things for babies, and maternity dresses and things like that.

'The yellow one?'

'No, the little pink one.' He looked again. 'The yellow one's all right too.'

'All right price tags,' I said, peering in. 'That one costs thirty quid.'

'Thirty quid!' He was amazed. 'For a dress for a baby?'

'Stupid, isn't it,' I said. 'This is a really posh bit of town, though.'

'So we can't get one for Iris?'

'Cal, we can't even afford to get her a dress from the supermarket.'

'Poor Iris,' he said.

'She's fine just in a vest. She doesn't know the differ-ence. Come on, Dad and Feng'll be waiting.'

Dad and Feng appreciated their ice lollies, and Dad was so glad to find Cal had shaken off his mood that he didn't bother telling him off any more. We drove home with Cal picking all the songs on the iPod and blasting them out so loud people glared at us in traffic.

Dad brought us to the front door but said he couldn't come in because he had to work in the afternoon. He gave us our pocket money, and Adam's too, and told us to say hi to Mum for him and tell her he was looking forward to tomorrow night. Cal and Feng kept giving me and each other knowing looks all the way into the kitchen.

Mum had been out for a walk, she said, and Adam was still out shopping for God knows what. I ate my lunch fast and went out to the shed – it was harder to think of excuses now exams were over.

Adam was inside the shed, which surprised me, with the curtains drawn, though the door was open. He looked up as I went in, his face pale in the gloom. 'You're back. Iris is sick.'

'What, really?' I asked, passing him the Kit Kat I'd brought to tide him over till he went in for lunch, and jumping over the piles of vests and nappies. He had the baby basket on the table. Iris had her eyes shut but she was tossing and turning from side to side.

'Feel how hot she is,' he said, ripping the wrapping off the Kit Kat and biting into it. I did. She was – maybe not burning up, but much hotter than she ought to have been. It was no time to panic, so I didn't. 'Right. What are we going to do?'

'I'm going inside. I'll go on the computer and find out.'

'Do you think she might just be, you know, too hot? It's boiling in here. Maybe I should take her outside, or give her a cool bath or something?'

We didn't know, that was the trouble, and even the Internet wasn't very helpful. Some websites said one thing and then someone else would say that would be fatal. What I wanted to do was ask Mum, or even better to hand Iris over so Mum could do it all. We did pull her basket out into the breeze after a bit, and flannelled her face and hands to try to cool her down. She drank most of the milk we gave her, though a lot of it came back up – I made a bottle of just water to see if that helped but she choked on it. She didn't cry all that much, in fact she was dozy all afternoon.

'Surely she'd be screaming more if she was really sick,' I said to Adam.

'I don't know,' he said.

She got hotter in the early evening, around dinner

time. I'd pinched the thermometer from the bathroom, though it didn't seem to be working very well. Kiran turned up around then too, and when he'd felt her he said he didn't think she was hot enough to really, really worry about, which was a relief because after a whole afternoon of it we'd lost our sense of proportion. 'We were half-thinking we should be dashing her to hospital.'

'I don't think she's that bad,' he said.

'Thank God for that.'

'But I do think you ought to take her to a doctor tomorrow.'

We stared at him in dismay. 'How are we supposed to do that?' Adam said. 'She's not in the system, and even if she was, what's a doctor going to say if we rock up with a baby? "Er, how old are you?"'

Kiran shrugged. 'We're going to have to find a way, though, because correct me if I'm wrong, but this plan of yours was meant to keep her out of danger.'

'He's right, Adam,' I said, after a deep breath. 'Babies can get really sick really quickly. If we can't think of a way to do it ourselves then we'll have to go to Mum and Dad.'

We looked at each other.

'If we do, that'll be it.'

'I know,' I said crossly. 'But we can't keep her if it's putting her at risk, can we? I'm telling you now, we're going to get Mum if we need to.'

'Hey, hey, not so hasty,' Adam said. 'We're all intelligent people, to different degrees. If we think hard we can do this, I have complete faith. In fact,' he added with a modest sort of cough, 'I've just sort of half thought of an idea.'

None of us much liked the plan we ended up with – Kiran kept trying to fancy it up and cover every possible loophole; he hadn't learned to ride his luck yet, Adam said, the way we had. Adam didn't like not being more involved, and I think he was a bit resentful that it was Kiran who was in a position to call up a glamorous girl and ask her for the favour we needed, but he was really anxious that the whole thing got done the best way possible – and also about getting to school on time the next day. He seemed to think if he didn't he'd have run over his limit and the teachers would come round with bloodhounds and magnifying glasses. As for me, I was petrified of messing up my part. But there wasn't much time to argue because Adam said the whole thing would probably take ages and we didn't want to be messing about trying to sort it all night.

The plan was that, once we'd rung NHS Direct and checked it would be OK not to do anything before morning, I would ring up this doctor's surgery we'd picked out of the phone book. We'd chosen it because it was miles away in a part of town where Adam happened to know his history teacher lived. We'd found her address in the phone book too and this was her closest doctor's so we were counting on her being registered there. I had to pretend to be her, on the phone.

'You're great at accents,' Kiran reassured me. 'I've heard you ... Isn't she?' he demanded.

'Yeah, she's all right,' Adam said.

'I saw you in the play, you were brilliant. Here, the phone's ringing.' He passed me the mobile. We were doing NHS Direct first.

'Oh, hello,' I said, in a posh, middle-aged woman's voice. 'I wonder if you could help me. I've got my niece staying at the moment with her baby and the child seems not to be well.' I described Iris's symptoms. 'No, it was a normal birth.' We all winced. We had no idea about the birth, except for knowing that it wasn't in a hospital. 'Yes, I'll be on this number. Thank you.'

While we were waiting for NHS Direct to get back to us on Adam's phone, I rang the out-of-hours surgery we'd picked on Kiran's. They were pretty helpful and said Iris would probably be all right till tomorrow. 'Oh, thank you,' I said, still in the voice, which was beginning to sound like the Queen. 'I don't suppose you would be able to book the appointment now, would you? Oh, wonderful, that will save her queuing up first thing tomorrow. Well, this is the thing – she's not actually registered at the surgery, they live in Kent, you see. Yes, they're staying with me. Mmm. Oh, thank you so much. And what will she need to fill in the form?' Kiran passed me a pen and a piece of paper. 'Right. No, I'm not sure if she's got that with her, actually. I'll ask her to bring it if she's got it, shall I? Well, thank you so much. Twenty to nine, yes.'

'Well done,' Kiran said.

'You didn't sound anything like her,' Adam said.

I rolled my eyes. 'I didn't have to sound like her, Adam, I was never going to sound like her, I've never met her.'

'If that receptionist had known her voice, we would have been screwed.'

'Yes,' Kiran snapped, 'and if it turns out tomorrow that the receptionist is her mother-in-law and knows she hasn't got a niece with a baby in Kent, we'll have to conclude that Fate was against us.'

That was the last of the arrangement-making phone calls. NHS Direct did ring back in the end but didn't have much to add, though it was nice to hear yet again that it didn't sound like an emergency and we were doing the right things so far.

Kiran had a laptop of his own but there was no Internet access in the shed or in his garden so even after things were settled, which was late, he kept going and then coming back with pieces of information.

That was the easy part, of course, though it had left me sweating. We knew that none of us was going to pass muster as someone who ought to be responsible for a baby. So we'd had to think of someone who would, and who wouldn't scream and report us to the police immediately, or else go round and tell all their mates.

'Shantel Hardwick?' I'd said. 'Do you think that's a good idea? Don't we want someone a bit less, er, noticeable?'

'No,' said Adam. 'We want someone so outlandish that they don't notice so much how old she is.'

'Or if they do think she looks young they also think they might be mistaken,' Kiran agreed, 'because she's strange. Anyway, it's not as if we can pick and choose. Do you know her, Phoebe?'

Of course I didn't know her. Actually I was sort of amazed that even Kiran did. I hadn't known that Adam had ever even heard of her, though she was a bit of a legend at my school. Once it had been sort of exciting, in a lame way, just to be in a scene in a play with her, and now she was apparently going to be right in the middle of this huge crisis in my life. Because she said yes to Kiran when he phoned her.

He'd said she would; he'd said she was constantly in pursuit of anything that would help her become an actress – of course I knew that she was going to be an actress, the whole school did, but I'd never heard it from someone who actually knew her before – and she would be happy to do him a favour.

Adam and I both slept in the shed because we thought something might happen that would need both of us and I was glad, not just of the help, but to be distracted. It was a bit frightening, especially when Iris started with a hacking cough. She was burning hot. Then she started retching at about two in the morning. I was going through the illness section in the biggest library book, squinting at it under the lamp. The worst things all seemed possible. 'What if she has a convulsion? She's boiling.'

'If she has a convulsion we'll go and get Mum,' Adam said, rocking her back and forth.

'If she has a convulsion, Adam, it might be too late to get Mum,' I shouted. 'Is that a rash on her arm?'

We banged heads checking, as he held her in the circle of light. 'I think she's just hot.'

'We need a glass. Why don't we have a glass?'

We gave her a coolish bath which seemed to help. She even slept for a bit then.

When it started getting light, Kiran came over the wall.

With it still being pretty dark it took all of us to get the pushchair over into the alley again, and then the baby. Then it took Adam to get me up the wall, and Kiran to get me down again. When I was finally getting my breath back, Adam hung over the top, peering down at us in the pitchy alleyway. 'For God's sake be careful. Stay out of sight till you meet your friend.'

'We will,' Kiran said. I'd been listening to it all night and was just ignoring him now.

'I'm sorry not to be coming, but I've got to get to school today or they'll be calling up Mum. And I'd just make you more noticeable.'

'We know. Don't worry, I'll take care of them.'

'And tell your friend to be careful as well. Especially her.'

The pushchair seemed to soothe Iris. She whimpered a bit every now and again when we went up and down kerbs but her eyes were closed and she was stiller than she had been in the night. It was strange walking through the lightening streets with the baby, and with Kiran. I'd wrapped a scarf round my head to hide my face so I wouldn't look so much like a kid, and was wearing a long skirt of Mum's, although I was afraid it just made me look like a small lumpen child. I looked down whenever we passed anyone, which wasn't all that often. Kiran seemed completely at ease, whistling and everything. 'You're in a good mood,' I said after a while.

'It's an act,' he said, smiling at a woman who'd glanced into the pushchair as she went by.

By the time it was really light and there were a few more people on the streets, we were getting right across town, close to the doctor's surgery we were heading for. There was a park opposite it that we were going to hide in, and a corner that wasn't near any gates and had a bench. Kiran left us there and went off to buy a coffee, he said. When he came back he had two bacon rolls, one for me, and a tea as well because I'd said I don't drink coffee. I don't actually, but I'd have said that anyway because I didn't want to waste cash when we might have to buy medicine, or something.

'I don't have any money,' I said. I was gruff because I was embarrassed. I did have money, too, and Kiran knew it, but I hoped he'd know what I meant.

'I know,' he said mildly. 'Don't worry about it.'

'Thanks.' I was starving. It felt like lunch time, even though it was only about seven o'clock. The bench had been soaking wet with dew when I sat down but I'd mopped most of it up with my skirt. I was really tired. Apart from anything else, it had been a really long walk. A woman walked by and sort of eyed us a bit suspiciously, but there was enough left of the bacon roll to hide some of my face, and Kiran just stared back. I leaned over the pushchair. Iris's hand was cool but when I felt her leg, under the blanket, it was still burning.

'Why don't you stretch out and have a bit of a kip?' he said when I was sipping the tea. 'She won't be here for another hour.'

'I'm fine.'

'Yeah, you look it. If anyone looks too closely they'll be calling Social Services for you, never mind Iris.'

'That's not funny,' I said, but I did curl up. He moved to the edge of the bench with his coffee to make room for me. I'd only closed my eyes and I was drifting off, but Iris woke up. She started crying again straight away, like she had in the night; it wasn't her loudest cry, but it was sort of hoarse and miserable and went through me even more than usual. She sounded so tired.

'I'll walk her round for a bit,' he said, getting up. 'See if she goes off again. Don't worry, I won't go too far.'

I wanted to pick her up and comfort her, but it hadn't worked in the night, we'd all been too hot, and she did seem to like the pushchair. I stayed awake until they passed me a few minutes later, walking up and down and around, and I could hear that she wasn't crying anymore. Kiran waved and I dropped off. I should have tried to hold on, because when I woke up he was standing right above me with Shantel Hardwick, and I had to sit up with my creased round face and silly long wet skirt while she towered over me. I wouldn't have thought she could stand out more than she did at school, but somehow in the park she looked even more so.

'Hi,' I said.

'Hi, Phoebe,' she said, and a month ago it would have

been a moment to treasure. 'It's gone half eight, shall we get going?'

'You're the one cutting it fine,' Kiran said.

'I got up really early actually. This is worse than school.' She held out her ballet-girl arms. 'Come on then, get her out for me.'

'Don't you want her in the pushchair?' I asked, too anxious to be calm. 'Do you know how to hold her properly?'

'I'm not going to drop her.'

'No, I know, but you've got to look like you're used to holding her.'

'I stand a better chance of that than looking as if I'm used to undoing the straps on that thing,' she said, taking Iris, who was half-awake. 'Come on, beautiful. Let's be having you . . . She doesn't look much like me.'

'No one looks like you, Shantel,' Kiran said. 'Martine Kramer, remember.' She'd already set off up the path and just waved her arm without turning round. After a minute we started following her, though we stopped as she went out of the gate and across the road to the surgery. I leaned against the fence. Kiran went to hide the pushchair a bit so we didn't look so odd.

The plan was that Shantel would take Iris into the surgery and fill in a form as a non-resident, pretending that they actually lived in Kent (where she attended a

201

surgery in Canterbury we'd found online), but they were staying down the road from here with her aunt. We were praying that Adam's history teacher used the surgery, if they checked, and that the doctor didn't know her well enough to know she didn't have a niece with a baby and volcanic hair.

We knew that they might have to wait a while to be seen, but it was only about five minutes before I started getting jumpy. There were so many things that could go wrong, all besides what the doctor might actually say about how ill Iris was. I would have much rather had time to coach Shantel properly, to make sure she had all the information they might need about the last few days, and Iris's whole life. I'd rather have had someone I felt I could coach. I'd rather have been able to take the baby in myself.

We stayed out of sight of the surgery windows, just in case anyone got suspicious of Shantel and started looking to see who might be waiting for her; but I could see the people who went in and out. There was a woman with a howling baby, much bigger than Iris, in a pushchair, who I might have felt sorry for except I was too busy hoping he wouldn't make Iris any sicker, and a couple a bit older than Mum and Dad holding hands, and an old lady shuffling as if her legs wouldn't bend in the middle. It was sad to think of all that might be going wrong for them, and how complicated people's lives were. I preferred it when all that bothered me about doctors' surgeries was how boring it was to wait in them.

It was only just five to nine when we saw Shantel float out, completely airy, shunting Iris up on her shoulder like she'd done nothing else all her life. She looked both ways and then crossed towards us. Kiran started backing the pushchair away. We waited for her halfway down the path near the pavilion. Iris was wide awake, looking at me with bright squirrel eyes from Shantel's narrow chest.

'Glad to put her down,' she said, rotating her shoulder while I stroked Iris's head. 'Bloody heavier than she looks.'

'Well?' I said.

'Doctor says don't worry too much. The rash is nothing, just heat or some kind of reaction, he could barely see it. Long as she's drinking and has wet nappies she's all right. Keep checking her temperature, he says you've got to get a proper thermometer, one of those you stick in their ears. He wrote down the temperature you've got to worry at and whip her into hospital, and some other stuff too. Here. And don't ignore your instincts. Well, my instincts.'

I gave a big sigh and hefted her up on my shoulder. I've never been so pleased with an anticlimax in my life. She snuffled into my neck and Kiran patted me on the back. 'How did it go, Shantel?'

'Piece of cake. I did the Kent address on the form, but they didn't check it. Of course, they might later, but I won't be there then so who cares. They asked me about a red book, so I just said I'd forgotten it.' I nodded. I'd heard of red books online. 'I saw they were a bit surprised but they never asked me how old I was, or anything. I suppose they get all sorts in there.'

'Not round here,' I said, looking through the trees at the big houses.

'Anyway he had a good prod of her, which she didn't seem to like much, and listened to her heart and looked in her ears and all that. She's good, for a baby, isn't she? And took her temperature. He said keep her in a cool room if you can, dry, with plenty of fresh air. And asked if I'd be going home in time for her to have her immunisations.'

'Oh God,' I said, 'there's another complication.'

'For another time,' Kiran said firmly. 'Come on, Shantel, you can buy us a thermometer before you go. There's a chemists just up there. And some day, if you're lucky, I'll tell you what it's all about.'

'Some day I might even be interested,' she said, patting his cheek.

Chapter Thirteen

Kiran insisted on walking us all the way home, in case anyone looked too hard at us or asked awkward questions, though actually I was beginning to believe that even if adults saw a bunch of kids in balaclavas fleeing down the street swinging a baby round their heads they'd look the other way and carry on on their way to work. I was glad to have him with us, but it was a bit embarrassing when I got sort of inadvertent surges of energy and started skipping along, without realising it, like I did when I was younger. We didn't talk most of the way, both having tired brains.

As we finally crossed over the river into our neighbourhood, he shook himself and said, 'Well, that's that. Shantel's something, hey?'

My stomach sank a bit but I was too tired to change the subject. 'She is. Did she really not want to know anything?'

'Well, I told her I couldn't explain. I think she would

reckon it would damage her mystique to beg. She plays it cool, I expect you've noticed.' We laughed.

'What was in it for her, then?'

He shrugged. 'New experiences. She likes doing strange things. And she's got nothing against helping people out, she's just not very interested in knowing about them.'

'Not like you,' I said. 'I don't know why you've been so good to us.'

He glanced down at me over his shoulder. 'I wanted to be a part of it. It's really huge, what you've been doing. It's – extraordinary. And you're extraordinary.' He patted me on the back. 'And your blush is extraordinary.'

It was nerve-racking letting myself into the house, just in case something had gone wrong and Mum or Dad was there, but it was completely empty. I made myself a drink. It had been really hot outside again, and even more sweaty than yesterday, though it was only about half past ten. The garden looked awfully bright, and the thought of spending another whole day in the hot shed with its stupid wooden floor was just a bit too much. Instead I left Iris in the pushchair, where she was just waking up, and belted out and got her basket and some of her things from the shed, then took the whole caboodle up to my bedroom. It gets hot at night, but during the day it's beautifully shady and cool, at least if you open the window and leave the door open too. It was just so comfortable being indoors. When Iris was having her feed we had the radio on, and when she slept in the afternoon I stretched out on my bed and had a snooze for an hour. I felt like everything was going to be all right.

She was still a bit miserable, though, choking on her bottles and crying in that hoarse way. After lunch I noticed that her sheet was all damp from sweat, and so was the vest she was wearing, which was a bit of a nightmare because, being a Monday, there was nothing clean – we just couldn't do any washing at weekends, Mum was never out long enough. I ended up using a T-shirt of Adam's as a sheet, and leaving nothing on her except a nappy.

I cut it too fine to get all of Iris's stuff back out to the shed before Dad came in with Feng and Cal; I had to leave most of it in my room, with the door carefully shut, and just pelt out with her quickly. Dad didn't stick around very long after Adam got back, he had things to do before he and Mum went out that evening; I was just waiting with Cal for Adam and Feng to come back and tell us the coast was clear, when there was a whistle in the alleyway and Kiran came dropping over the wall.

I told him how the day had gone, and he said it was probably a good sign, her sweating so much; it would bring her temperature down, and at least she wasn't dehydrated — not yet, anyway. He actually took her off me and sat with her against his chest for a while. Iris looked gravely across at me as if to say she trusted me but she wasn't sure what was going on. Cal was doing handstands against the shed, and just as Adam came panting round the corner with Feng, he fell and managed to kick out a little pane of glass from the door.

'Brilliant,' I said, 'a hole in the shed. Just what we need.'

'You can fix it,' Cal said anxiously.

'Don't worry about it now,' Adam said, which was unlike him. 'How was today?'

I'd already spoken to him on the phone that morning, he'd rung from school to find out how Iris was, but he hadn't had time for the details. We gave him a rundown now, although he seemed distracted. 'I think she's probably getting better,' I told him. 'She feels cooler than she did this morning.'

'That's great. Now, the thing is, there was a bit of a development today. When I rang up your school to tell them you wouldn't be in, the woman on the phone was a bit tight-lipped with me, if you know what I mean.'

'Not really,' I said cautiously.

'I mean, I got the feeling that there was a bit of a question mark hovering over you, and that if I'd pushed it a bit, which I probably would have done if I'd really been Dad, she would have got into it with me. Now, it seems a bit weird. I know you've missed some days lately, but you were in all last week, so why are they suspicious? Do you think it could be about your exams?'

I shrugged. 'I told you they didn't go well.'

'Yeah, but I thought you were exaggerating. Were they bad enough to start them wondering?'

'I don't know.' I felt uncomfortable, partly because they were all looking at me.

'It's just, even if they don't feel the need to ring up Mum and Dad about it, if Mum or Dad should get in touch with them for any reason it might all come out, how many days you've missed and stuff. And I think it's going to be pushing your luck to take any more time off at the moment.'

'So are you going to do it?'

'Well, I'm kind of in the same boat,' he said in a worried voice. 'Today Mr Goldstein said I looked remarkably healthy for someone who was off school all last week.'

'So what are we going to do?'

He looked at Kiran. 'I was wondering if you felt like skipping a day, mate,' he said. 'Or possibly two.'

I looked at Kiran as well. His eyes were down on the grass, or on Iris's little round feet, which weren't scaly

209

anymore, resting against his belt. A shaft of sunlight struck almost blue against his hair, though his face was in the shade. He picked a little bug off Iris's knee.

'No,' he said. 'I don't think so.'

'No?'

'No.'

'Got a bit of a record, too, have you?' I wasn't sure if Adam was joking to avoid sounding disappointed, or angry.

'No, I haven't. But I think it's over, guys.'

'What?' I said. Kiran had helped out so much, he'd been with me all that morning and even come home with me to make sure we were all right, and now I couldn't believe the expression on his face.

'Look, you've run the, what do you call it, the gauntlet for a while, you've done really well. Seriously, I take my hat off to all of you. But sooner or later, and I'd say sooner from the way things are going, you're going to have to give it up and tell your parents, or tell someone. You know you are, you admit it. And now, she's been ill and you've got her better, but it's a bit of a warning, isn't it? Why not just accept it before something else happens?'

'We can't do that. What, just give her up like she's a puppy we found in the street?'

'It's the only thing you can do in the end, and it might turn out great,' Kiran said gently, not looking at me but at

Cal and Feng. 'I bet she'll be adopted straight away by some nice couple who'll think she's the best thing ever.'

'We think she's the best thing ever,' Adam said stiffly, reaching forward and taking Iris from him.

'And it doesn't work like that,' I shouted, frustrated.

'They'll take her into Care,' Cal said in a completely betrayed-sounding voice.

'Well...' He paused. 'Would that be so terrible, necessarily? I mean, you two are all right, here, aren't you? It's not horrible for you?'

'You think all foster homes are like this?' Cal asked. 'You don't know *anything*.'

'Granted. But I'm afraid of what might happen if you keep going and, you know, I just don't see what you have to gain by it because, in the end, you can't go on like this.' He looked around at us all. 'I was in it up till now because I thought it was such a massive thing, and I do believe you about why you want to do it. But it won't do, and you know it. Someone's going to find out, and whatever's going to happen is going to happen however long you've managed to hide her. Look at you, you're worrying about missing school – and she's still not well, and you've got to keep her in a horrible little shed, with a hole in the door, all day in this sweltering weather. How's she going to get well properly? I just think you're taking risks, with her, for no good reason now. So I'm out.'

'What do you mean, *you're out*?' Adam asked.

'I'm not going to tell anyone. It's your thing. And I think you'll see it yourselves anyway, before too long. I'm not going to come here anymore. If you need me for anything, you know where I live.'

'We don't, actually,' Adam muttered. I couldn't look but I felt Kiran glance round at all of us before he got up and walked away. Adam said, louder, 'Well, thanks for today, anyway,' and I heard the scuffle of Kiran swinging himself up in the tree, then I rolled over and lay on my face on the grass.

I felt more abandoned than I had done since the whole thing started. I heard Feng trying not to cry, and Iris beginning to whimper.

After a bit Adam got up and walked about with her. 'Look,' he said suddenly, in a strong voice. 'Cheer up, everyone. Mum'll be back soon, and she'll be getting ready to go out with Dad. We want her nice and cheerful, so tails up. Feng, stop crying. Phoebe.'

'Yes.'

'He was right about one thing. You kept her in the house today, didn't you?'

'Yes.'

'Was it better?'

'Yes,' I admitted.

'Right. Well, whatever about taking risks, she's not

212

well and we need to do the right thing to look after her properly. So after Mum goes out tonight we're going to bring her into the house, and keep her there.'

'All night?' I asked faintly.

'Yep.'

'Without Mum finding out?'

'Look, we're going to have to be brave about this, right? He who dares wins. It's not as ludicrous as it sounds, Phoebe. Your room's well away from Mum's, it's the other end of the corridor.'

'Yeah, but in this heat she'll have all the doors open.'

'That's the thing. You know how soundly she sleeps when she's had a few.'

'You don't know even know they'll be drinking.' Mum's not a heavy drinker usually. The night Dad moved out I found her in the kitchen at half past eleven staring at a glass of whisky and an almost-full bottle. Save alcohol for the good times, she'd told me. Don't waste it on the bad, or it makes things worse.

'You know that when she and Dad used to go out, they always had a bottle of wine and that was always all it took for Mum.' It was true, and things had gone well the last few times they'd seen each other. But what if they argued after all tonight? Then she'd be home early, and extra prickly.

'It's a risk worth taking,' Adam said when I pointed that

out, and I agreed because I was tired, and for once I was glad for him to take charge, and it didn't feel right to be the one saying no, let's keep our sick baby in the hot shed instead of in a nice house for the night.

So Adam sat with Iris most of the early evening, and I watched the boys in the front room while Mum got ready; they were incredibly good about being put to bed and then off Mum went, looking all lovely in a top I hadn't seen before and the shoes Dad bought her for her birthday once, and an absolute cloud of perfume. Then Cal and Feng got up again and we brought Iris in, and her basket, and since she was going to be in the whole night, almost all her things. I got a wash on as well, and dressed her in one of the vests which were finally dry.

Probably last night was the night we should have done this, I thought as I ran the bath, since she was getting better now; but then, Mum hadn't been out and had been completely sober. Anyway it was sort of nice just being us lot again, and not having to explain anything or argue with someone outside the family; that's what I told myself. Since Iris was all that mattered, it was good not to be worrying about the impression I was making on anyone else.

We all sat round and watched TV until it became completely unsuitable for Feng and Cal, and then we went upstairs to Feng's room and played cards. They wouldn't go to sleep before Mum came back, so I hoped Mum would be a bit less alert than usual. She'd probably want to scamper round giving everyone smoochy kisses goodnight but at least she wouldn't be as likely to notice them completely overacting being asleep.

Iris had got so that after her ten o'clock bottle she was good for a few hours' sound sleep most nights, and though she was still hot she was so tired we thought once she was properly in her basket she'd stay there for a while, so we'd put her in my bedroom and just left the door open so we'd hear her if she woke up. At eleven o'clock we insisted on leaving the boys upstairs; Cal was mostly asleep already leaning against Adam, and didn't even mind being lifted into bed. It was just as well we moved downstairs because ten minutes later Mum came home, humming to herself, throwing her shoes into the corner as she got through the door, and delighted rather than cross to find us up waiting for her. We had music playing, and as I got up to slide out and shut the door to my bedroom, she seized hold of me round the waist and made me dance with her.

'I take it you had a good night,' Adam said, shutting the front-room door instead.

'It was nice,' she agreed, dreamily swinging me round.

'You and Dad got on all right, then?'

She collapsed onto the sofa. 'Don't be in a rush, OK? It's not the kind of thing you should rush, even if you could.

But we did have a lovely time. And it's even lovelier, or just as lovely, to come home to my angels.'

'Do you want a drink, Mum?' Adam asked from the corner where the globe is, the one they keep the booze in.

'Oh, I've had enough.'

'Not at all. Look, I'm holding it already. Gin and tonic?'

'Well, you're being very sweet tonight,' she said in grateful surprise, sinking back into the cushions. 'Has something happened that's going to cost me money?'

'No, no,' I said soothingly. I could see Adam trying to squeeze some tonic into the glass. 'Tell us about your evening.' She did, for a while. Once she'd got used to the drink and the glass was emptying, Adam went off to lock up, and have a peep at the three little ones. Mum leaned across to me on the sofa and pulled me into her arms.

'I don't know what I'd do without you, Phoebe,' she said, 'you know that, don't you? My beautiful girl. You're my sunshine and my comfort, you know that, don't you?'

''Course,' I said, patting her on the back.

'And if there's ever anything you need to talk about,' she said into my shoulder, 'you can come to me, you know that? Whatever it is.'

'I know,' I said. I felt tearful. She was just being a bit sentimental, but I felt terrible sometimes about keeping something like this from her. It wasn't just hiding the truth, or even knowing that whenever she did find out about it she'd be really hurt that we hadn't come straight to her – it was that the things we were doing, even though she didn't know about them, did make her life just that bit more difficult. That jug we'd pinched, the sun cream that she had to get for Cal because he burned so easily and that we'd nicked because we couldn't keep Iris completely out of all sunshine – she'd spent ages searching for the bottle, and had to buy a new one in the end – and just the fact that we didn't have time to be there for her, any of us, if she needed any help or someone to talk to... Anyway, I felt terrible.

The night went all right. Adam had been spot on – all Mum wanted to do was sleep once she'd finished the drink he made her. When she was asleep we shut her door as quietly as we could. Adam didn't sleep in my room because there actually wasn't enough space on the floor with all Iris's things everywhere, but he told me to call him if I needed him. But Iris was much better. She never got very hot again and she only woke up twice.

The morning was a bit of a rush – I went into Mum's room early, just before her alarm went off, to keep her chatting while Adam took Iris and her basket out to the shed. There wasn't any hurry, actually; Mum just lay there, death groaning about how exhausted she was, until the absolute last minute before we'd all have been late for school and work. I offered to make the lunch boxes and she nearly kissed me again. We'd decided Adam would risk the next couple of days off, and I'd go into school, take the telling off I thought I might get for messing up exams – or the series of tellings off – and tomorrow try to look a bit sick so I could be off for the next few days without it being too suspicious. Adam was on holidays after this week so if we could just hold off till then we'd be OK.

'Now we don't know what they're going to throw at you,' Adam said as I scrabbled my stuff together in the shed before leaving, 'so just try and think on your feet, and get out of it without making them think too much about anything.'

I felt like a spy, walking into school, like I needed to try to avoid anyone over the age of eighteen, not to mention Kiran, and act completely nonchalant, while it was all I could do to keep my eyes open properly and be ready to smile. I had this terrified feeling that if anyone did pick on me, or even just ask why I'd planked one or other of my exams, I might burst into tears.

Actually it wasn't at all brutal. My form teacher looked relieved to see me and took me aside to ask if I was all right, and had I been ill. I said, well, yes, a bit, before exams, and then yesterday I'd just had a nasty bug. She warned me that my exam results might not all be as good as I'd like, since some of my teachers had been disappointed. 'They weren't terrible, I don't think,' she reassured me, 'but it's just we've come to expect the best from you, really, Phoebe.' That was the first I'd heard of it. She asked again if things were OK at home – she knows, of course, that I've got foster brothers. She folded her arms and put her head on one side, and when I said, feeling really ashamed of myself but just needing to get out of that room, that Dad had moved out a while ago, she got this very concerned expression. 'And so do you think that that affected your concentration?'

'Maybe, when I was revising,' I said, looking at the floor.

'Is it something you'd like to talk about?'

'No thank you,' I said quickly. 'Actually things have been much better for about a week now, so I'm really feeling fine.'

'All right. Well, why don't we wait and see what all your results actually are. If any of the other teachers want to talk about them, you let me know, OK, and we can all have a chat.'

None of them did. It seemed I'd scraped by enough not to get any talkings-to myself, though I thought my next Parents' Evening might not be much fun. They were a bit shocking, the results. Even before I'd taken the exams I could have guessed things like French and geography and science would be bad, because I just hadn't done enough revision, but I should have done OK in something like maths, because generally you can either do it or you can't. But I'd just been too tired even to concentrate for an hour and a half. I thought English had probably been fine, but I didn't have English that day so I didn't find out. The whole thing was a bit exhausting.

I sat on the edge of the football field by myself at lunch time, and I couldn't even be bothered to open a book and pretend I was reading. I just lay back and shut my eyes. Everything was red because of the sun.

'Phoebe?' a voice asked. I opened my eyes and it was Lily Buckley again. She looked hesitant. I said hi. She sat down next to me. 'I've been wanting to apologise.'

'You already did.' I felt a bit like how I imagine being drunk feels, like I couldn't control what I said like I normally do, or at least I didn't want to.

'Yeah, I mean, for that. Apologise for apologising.' We both laughed. 'Because I felt like I really embarrassed you.'

'You did. But don't worry. I've been meaning to say – I like your hair.'

She tucked a strand of it back and looked puzzled. 'I had it cut at Christmas.'

'Yeah. I've been meaning to say it – for a while.' My words were coming out slowly.

She smiled at me. 'I think it makes my ears look big.' It did make her ears look big. She had big ears and big eyes and a big mouth, and a thin clever face – she was thin and clever-looking all over actually. 'You look so tired,' she said, watching me. 'Everyone's been saying. I saw you nearly fall asleep in French today.'

'I didn't.'

'You did. Every time you blinked it was like you had to wrench your eyes open. Were you hitting the books really hard last week? What?' I had started laughing, weakly, but so much I was shaking. 'You're not secretly taking loads of drugs or something, are you?' I laughed at that so much I rolled over, and she laughed too, lying on the grass beside me. 'I notice you haven't answered my question.'

'Yes, I'm a secret drug-head. That's exactly what it is.'

'You're a mystery anyway. Listen, it's my birthday soon. A bunch of us are going shopping on Saturday, and my dad's going to give me some money so we can go for lunch somewhere. Do you want to come?'

'I can't,' I said. I didn't worry about sounding regretful enough because I was regretful. 'There's all this stuff going on at home.'

'Yeah?'

I probably could have got away for a few hours, for something important, but what was the point really? I was just too busy. 'Yeah, sorry.'

'S'OK. Some other time.' She smiled at me as she got up and wandered off.

I was hot when I got home, so hot that I stopped in the kitchen to get a drink before I went and threw my sweaty uniform off and had a shower. Feng had made a jug of Ribena with ice in it. I drained one glass and sat down at the table with another. Dad came in from the front room, where Cal and Feng were watching their after-school TV. 'How was your day, lovey? Did you get more of your results? Were they good?'

I was tired of the pointless lies. There were enough point-full ones. 'So-so,' I said. 'I didn't revise enough. There was too much going on.'

'Like what?' he asked, surprised, sitting down with me. I reached behind him and shut the kitchen door.

'Like you and Mum, and all that. But last night went well, didn't it? Are you thinking of moving back in?'

Dad looked really surprised now. He coughed. 'You can't rush these things, you know, Phoebe. You've got to give your mum and me enough time to come to the right decision for both of us.'

'I know, Dad, and I know it's your decision, yours and Mum's, but it affects all of us, a lot.'

'Of course it does,' he said, on safer ground. 'We know that.'

'Obviously it affects any kids when their parents are

thinking about maybe splitting up, but it's worse for us, especially those two.' I nodded at the door. 'They're only six and eight, and they're worrying not just about their dad leaving, but whether that means they'll have to leave too, and get chucked back in the system.'

'That's not going to happen.'

'Tell them that.'

He was looking at me in a very questioning way. I was about ready for that shower now; my stomach was full of ice. 'I didn't know you worried so much about Cal and Feng.'

'They're my family,' I said. I stood up. 'Frankly, Dad, I don't mean to be disrespectful, but I think you need to man up and come to some decisions.'

It was a bit dangerous talking to Dad that way, if only because it was rocking the boat and making both him and Mum – I'm sure he told Mum all about it as soon as she got home – more likely to want to find me, corner me and talk to me; but I was fed up with trying to be so grown-up all the time and make the right decisions when he wasn't bothering to pull his weight. And it wasn't just me. The little boys were tired just from living at the pitch they had been, on their nerves all the time. And Adam looked shattered when I went out to the shed, with black rings round his eyes, even though he said Iris was completely better and had been happy as a trout all day. 'Full of smiles,' he said, 'whereas I'm full of cold.'

'Not you, now, too,' I said.

'Yeah, but never mind. How were your results?'

It got cooler that evening, though the sky was still cloudless. I was glad we could keep the baby in the shed again without worrying about the heat, and without having to have a storm or something to break the weather. That hole in the door might be a problem if it really rained.

It was just as well we hadn't got cocky and tried keeping her in the house again, because Mum was up a couple of times that night. I heard her and wondered what she was doing, but guessed Cal must be sick because she seemed to be going in and out of his room.

She told me in the morning he had a nasty temperature as well as a blocked head. I went out to tell Adam he'd have to be specially careful, since Mum would be in all day looking after Cal.

It was a scorcher too, and all day while everyone wilted around me and flinched away from wasps, I looked out of the classroom windows at the bright blue sky and thought about Adam and Iris sweating in that shed, maybe not even able to lie outside in case Mum was getting a breath of fresh air or looking out of a window upstairs. I worried again and again about whether Kiran was right and all we were doing was delaying the inevitable and giving Iris and everyone else a really nasty time while we did it.

I didn't wait for anyone when school was over, I just ran home, and bought Adam an ice lolly on the way. I was a bit early, having run, so instead of going through the house and having to stop and chat before I could make an excuse to go out, I went up the alleyway. After the last time, Adam and Kiran had piled a few more big stones and bricks there, and it was easy enough to scramble up the wall on my own, though the lolly took a battering.

Adam had the door wide open, and it wasn't too stuffy in there, though he'd kept the baby in just a nappy and didn't have his own T-shirt on. He was glad of the mashed lolly. 'Where'd you get the money?'

'It was what was left after the last pack of nappies. How've you been?'

He made a face. 'I'll be glad to get back to school, put it that way. We'll have to talk about what we're doing tomorrow, and till the end of the week.'

It was just then that we heard a bang, like a door hitting brickwork, and Mum shouting at the other end of the garden and then, worst of all, feet running. We looked at each other for a second with stretched eyes, then Adam leaped to his feet and out of the shed, slamming the door shut. Luckily the curtains were pulled. I crouched over the baby, ready to snatch her up if she cried.

'Mum!' he said, 'what's the matter?'

I heard Mum's voice, as if she'd just come round the corner. She sounded frantic. 'Do you know where Cal is?'

'No,' Adam said. 'I thought he was sick.'

'He was, but he's not in his bed, I don't know where he is. He can't possibly have got out of the house without me seeing, but he's not there. I don't know what to do. Oh Christ. Come and help me look for him.' She paused. 'What are you doing, home at this time?'

'I was just a bit early, so I came out here...'

'Not through the house, I didn't see you.' Her voice was nearer. 'What's going on here? Adam, tell me the truth.'

'I am.'

'Do you know where Cal is?'

'No, but I'll help you look.'

'Tell me the truth, Adam. Is he in that shed?'

'No, no he's not. Mum, don't—' The door handle was turning.

'Get out of my way, Adam,' she said, and she came into the shed.

Chapter Fourteen

Weeks afterwards, when I could think a bit more clearly about it all, I thought Mum handled it pretty well, considering. I mean, she'd gone upstairs to find her sick six-year-old was missing completely, come running into the garden to find her half-naked son was standing in front of the shed as if it had a dead body in it, then busted in and found her daughter huddled on the floor clutching a five-week-old baby. It probably felt like about her worst nightmare. But she didn't scream or have to grab anything to stop herself collapsing, though she definitely went pale; I watched the colour drain out of her face like in books.

I lost my head and blurted out, 'She was Leanne's!' before she could even ask.

'Leanne's?' she whispered.

'Leanne left her here with us,' Adam said. He seemed quite calm, although he was pale too. Mum looked from us to him. 'She wanted you to keep her. But we were afraid that, with Dad not living here, you wouldn't be allowed to. So we've been looking after her.'

'For how long?' Mum asked wildly. We started to tell her the story, or Adam did; I kept jumping in with things. I didn't exactly know how to stop myself, even though he was giving me warning looks. I think he didn't want to shock her too much at once. But he hadn't got very far into it before she suddenly said, 'No, wait. Where's Cal?'

'I don't know,' Adam said, and I shook my head.

'Where was he meant to be?'

'In bed. I put him there after lunch – his temperature was up – and then when I went to check on him just now...I thought he was being quiet, oh God – he's nowhere in the house. But I don't understand how he got out; I was working in the kitchen, the front door was locked...'

'The tree,' I said; I thought I was going to be sick. I was still holding Iris though, so I swallowed it back.

'The tree?' Mum screamed. 'He climbed down that bloody tree? He's not well! He's six years old! Oh God, I've got to call the police. Come back to the house, *now*, both of you. And bring that child.'

'We wouldn't leave her behind,' I said, but she'd raced off. Adam went after her, leaving me to scramble up anyhow with the baby.

Mum was standing in the kitchen with her hands pressed to her face, looking at the phone. 'I've got to call them, haven't I? For a missing child. But God, what are Social Services going to say about all this? And you two! Give me that baby,' she said. Iris had started crying. I wanted to hold onto her but Mum's face was creasing up so I handed her over.

Adam was nearest the door to the front room, and just then he looked towards the window. 'Dad's back.'

Mum absolutely raced out of the house with Iris clutched to her chest; if she wasn't holding a baby I think she would have hurled herself on Dad, who was just getting out of the car. From inside I watched her gibbering at him. Feng's face was pressed anxiously against the car window. There was someone else in there too, in the front passenger seat, peering out – Feng's mother. There didn't seem to be much chance we were going to be able to keep this quiet.

It all happened at once really, or that's how it felt, so we can't have been worrying about Cal for long. Dad made the call to the police, mercifully, for it might have finished Mum off. When he put the phone down he told us they already had Cal; he'd been shoplifting in the posh baby clothes shop at the other end of town.

I still can't see how he managed to get there, through the city centre, without anyone stopping him. They noticed him all right as soon as he went in the shop; apparently he was wandering round all dazed, with his high temperature, and then tried stuffing a dress into his T-shirt. He was too sick to run very far before they caught him. When they couldn't find any parents they had to call the police.

So he came home in a police car, without the siren or the blue light admittedly. They said they hadn't been able to give him much of a talking-to because he was completely glazed over.

In the meantime Dad had called Stephen; he said Social Services would be in it from the start, and we might as well be the ones to call them. Stephen arrived lickety-split, he must have been nearby already, but he was just there, he wasn't saying anything at all. Mum was making huge pots of tea and Dad was taking Cal up to be washed and put to bed when Kiran busted through the door. He said he'd heard Mum in the garden and then seen the police car rolling by and had we thought about ringing the local paper because he was sure they could angle a story to get us the sympathy vote and it might make all the difference.

Mum had got over the worst of it when she heard Cal was OK, and was being quite business-like about getting everyone the right cup of tea, though she kept looking at me giving the baby a bottle; they all kept looking at us. Mum shushed Kiran and soothed him and told him everything was all right, that Social Services only had everyone's best interests at heart and he wasn't to worry. She said she and Dad were in on it now and they'd make sure anything that happened would work out.

I knew what that meant. I'd heard it over and over again, at times when kids arrived or left; she'd said it to me and to them, and so had Dad. They'd said there had to be rules, that otherwise no one would know that the best decision was being made; that without guidelines no one person was qualified to judge things like whether a child should live with its parents. They'd said it was all a co-operation, that they had to work with the government and with everyone to keep children safe. They'd said the rules were right and that the truth was the most important thing of all. Now she meant that we were going to lose Iris, but that it was for the best because we were just kids and she and Dad weren't sure what was happening with them right now, and that someone wise at Social Services would put her somewhere she would be looked after. I screamed.

They were all fussing round me, pointlessly, trying to get me to hand over Iris, which I had no intention of doing, till Adam got down in front of me and looked me in the eyes and said he'd hold her till I was ready to take her back. But Stephen, though he let Adam take her, said there were things that had to be checked before we could all relax. He stopped Mum trying to hug me and sat on the sofa beside me, but facing me, blocking Feng's mother who was watching from the corner of the room and clutching Feng's hand. 'The first thing for us to do is get the baby checked to make sure she's all right.'

'She is all right,' I said. There were tears streaming down my face, and it hurt. 'She wasn't very well a few days ago but we took her to the doctor, and she's better now.'

'You took her to the doctor?' Stephen shook his head. 'There's a lot for us to understand here, Phoebe, you can see that, can't you?' He looked at me. 'This is a very unusual situation. But if, as Adam says, she wasn't even born in a hospital, then she definitely needs to be checked over. We're not saying that you haven't looked after her properly. Though how you knew how to do it is beyond me. But we have to make sure she's OK first.'

'Can I go too?'

'No, not yet. You've got a lot to tell us, you and Adam.'

'Don't take her away,' I wailed.

'We're not taking her away, nothing like that is happening yet, no decisions are being made,' he said very seriously.

'Leanne wanted us to keep her. She wanted Mum and Dad to have her.'

'I know, Phoebe, but there's going to have to be a lot done before we can possibly start thinking about what will happen next. You're clearly in a difficult place right now –

you all are,' he said, looking round the room. Adam was standing in the corner with Iris up on his shoulder, half turned away from us. Feng was holding his mother's hand. Kiran was hunched up on one of the hard chairs Mum had brought in from the little room. Mum and Dad were standing side by side in front of the fireplace.

'It's my fault,' Dad said suddenly. 'Everything's been so disjointed lately.'

'Our fault,' Mum said, looking sideways at him. 'I still don't understand how this can have happened without me knowing, I don't feel like I've been neglecting them that much – we haven't had a chance to talk about this ourselves, Stephen, you know.'

'One thing you should know, before you do make any decisions,' I heard Dad say, because I couldn't look at them anymore, I couldn't deal with them being upset, 'is that funnily enough the situation that I suppose has led to this – me being away, I mean, the separation – I don't mean that Gillian hasn't been looking after them properly, but just – they've all been upset, I don't think we realised how much...'

'Spit it out, Richie,' Mum said.

'I'm coming home,' Dad said. 'We're back together.'

'That's right,' Mum said quickly. Adam had turned towards them, and I heard Feng take a breath, but I couldn't be excited.

'Well, that's great. Congratulations,' Stephen said, letting go of my hand which he had been holding tightly. 'I'm very pleased for you.'

'Yes, we're pleased too. We seem to have had a flurry of activity today just to usher in the new era,' Mum said brightly, 'but it's all back on, the marriage and everything, so things can get back to normal. And a new baby is actually just what we need, isn't it, Richie? A spanking new challenge. Keep us on our toes.'

'It's not quite as easy as that, Gillian,' Stephen said with a grin, 'as well you know. But thanks for making your position clear. Now, Adam, I'm going to have to ask you to give the baby to Denise. She's going to take her to the hospital just to make sure she's OK. I promise you,' he said, since Adam hadn't moved, 'this won't be it. We're not going to take her away and never let you see her again.'

Denise, who was another social worker apparently, was driven off with Iris in the police car. I stood by the window watching them go and there was such an ache in my chest that I only half-knew about the big fuss that was going on with making arrangements.

Cal was flat out upstairs now without a clue about what was going on, but of course, he had to have someone in the house looking after him. They got one of the neighbours in the end, Maria from down the street, who used to babysit for us sometimes.

Eventually I found myself in another police car with Dad, Adam and Stephen. I don't know how Feng and his mother got to the police station but they arrived just after us. While we were waiting for more people to turn up who apparently wanted to talk to us, Kiran came into the police station with his dad, who looked completely nonplussed. They sat down opposite me and Kiran smiled but I couldn't smile back.

There were three different people in the little room I got called into. I lost track of who was from Social Services and who was the police, it didn't seem that important. Dad wasn't there, I don't know if he was with Adam or with Feng, but Stephen came in and sat with me. They weren't at all nasty, they weren't even cross, but I kept feeling that they didn't believe me. They didn't seem to believe that Leanne had just turned up out of nowhere, that we'd had no contact with her before. They asked again and again about how we could have kept it all from Mum, and then, once they did believe she hadn't known, they wanted to know why we hadn't told her. I don't know what they expected me to say, that she was a terrible mother or something. 'We thought she wouldn't be allowed to keep Iris,' I kept saying, 'because of my dad not being there, and we didn't want her to go into Care.'

'But you must have known you couldn't continue like this for ever.'

'We did.'

'Did you think you were fit to look after her? Four children with no experience of babies, no money?'

'No, but we were scared to lose her.'

'Why?'

'Because we love her,' I shouted. I scared myself, shouting in a police station, but no one looked angry or like they were going to lock me away.

It felt like hours and I was trying desperately not to look too tired or too upset, because I wanted it sorted, I didn't want them to say, let's leave it till tomorrow, or next week, because I was only a child and they felt sorry for me. I had to hold up a bit longer so that we could get it all over with. I knew Adam would be doing the same, and probably Feng as well, if they were talking to him.

'It wasn't really anything to do with Feng, or Cal,' I said to them. 'It was only me and Adam at first, till they found out, and they just wanted to help. We didn't make them or anything, they just wanted to. But we tried not to let it affect them too much.'

'Only they love her too now,' Stephen suggested.

'Why did you call the baby Iris?' one of them, the big dark woman, asked me. She sounded genuinely interested. I couldn't figure out if I'd got them on my side, or if it was a trick question, and I didn't want to look like I was wondering if I could trust them.

236

'Because she's the goddess of the rainbow,' I said, starting to cry again.

I didn't know how I was doing anymore, I was so tired, but eventually everyone went away except Stephen, and I was beginning to think he was the one I could trust, though I knew that was dangerous. I rested for a long time and watched him writing a lot of stuff down. 'Where's my mum?' I asked him in the end.

'She went with the police to try and find Leanne,' he told me.

'What for?'

He put his pen down. 'We need to make sure she's not in trouble, first and foremost. Even you guys don't know what her situation was.'

'What if she says she wants Iris?'

'I don't think you need to worry about that,' he said, but I didn't know if he meant it wouldn't happen or just that it wasn't my place, anymore, to be worrying.

After another long time the door opened and Dad came in with Adam. Adam looked exhausted but he nodded at me and I nodded at him. Dad came over to my chair and picked me up, which he hasn't done for years. He had to put me down again almost straight away, but he kept his arm round me. 'Time to go home at last.'

'Where's Feng?' I asked him.

'He went back a while ago, his mother took him. Mum's at home now.'

'Did they find Leanne?'

'Yes. Everything's going to be fine. Come on.'

I couldn't bring myself to wonder about anything anymore, I just followed him. Adam was silent too. There was a taxi waiting for us outside, which was good because I hadn't brought a cardigan or anything and I was shivering in the night air. Normally in a black cab I like to sit on the jump seats, but I was too floppy and they put me on the long seat with Adam. I didn't wonder why Stephen was coming home with us till Adam asked him.

'I left my car parked outside your house,' Stephen said mildly. 'Anyway, I wanted to be there when you got home.'

'Why?' I asked. I had my eyes shut, I was so tired.

'Because I suspect your mum will have kept the baby up to wait for you.'

Adam sat up so fast I nearly slid off the shiny taxi seat. Stephen smiled. 'By all accounts she's fine, though I'm sure she should be in bed by now.'

I didn't say anything because I didn't want to ask anything more just then, and anyway I couldn't. It was like taking a huge deep breath when you come up from underwater, and your face almost hurts with it. I just leaned against my window, and Adam leaned against his, and watched the streets go past. It was like coming home from a war; everything looked different.

We got out of the car and waited for Dad to pay the driver, and all three of us walked close together to the front door. Stephen came behind. Mum met us in the hall with Iris in her arms. She looked at both me and Adam, and Adam stood back. I knew even at the time it was big of him to do that and that I couldn't have done it. I would have fought him if he'd tried to take her first.

'She was crying herself into a state at the hospital, poor lamb,' Mum said, watching me holding her, 'and all the way home, Denise said. But she relaxed a bit when I brought her in here, and I had a bottle ready. Apparently all the doctors and nurses had to say was what a lovely job you've done of looking after her.'

I wasn't allowed to hold her for long. Mum sent us both off to bed, she said the bags under our eyes were a disgrace. Anyway, Iris had been asleep for a while and she needed to be in her basket. Mum had moved it, and all the baby things, into her bedroom. 'I certainly won't be lonely in there tonight,' she said to me on the landing as I was coming back from brushing my teeth; Dad had gone in ahead of her.

Everything was so loaded for a while. We were tripping over social workers, mostly Stephen, luckily, for ages, and

I felt guilty about bringing that on the family, but they left us alone in the end, almost as much as before.

I think it took Mum and Dad a long time to get over what had happened, with us I mean. They seemed to feel like the conversation was never over. But it was hard for us to talk about; it was easier when they talked about other things, like what was going on with Leanne, though we never did find out all the details. That was fine with me. They'd found her very quickly anyway so I guess she hadn't gone off somewhere like she told us she was going to, but apparently she didn't exactly need rescuing; they said it was all a bit of a mess but Leanne was fine and safe, that she'd be looked after and that she still didn't want the baby, that she wanted Mum and Dad to have her. I felt so thankful to her, I couldn't have imagined.

They all kept telling us not to worry, that was the upshot of everything. Mum and Dad, and all the different people from Social Services, and my teachers, all wanted us to Talk About It but Not To Worry. They had a lot of material, it was true, with all the lies we'd told and why we hadn't felt able to ask for help, and the truanting (they called it), and all the deception, not to mention dragging Feng and Cal into it. Then, for ages, we had to go to counselling with professionals, all four of us. Kiran wanted to know why he didn't get to go too, since he was in on the secret as well, but Mum said he was the most well-adjusted person she knew.

I liked my counsellor, Christina. She mostly talked sense, even though some of it was hard to hear. It was hard to accept it when she said that, even though I'd done so well looking after Iris, that level of commitment was unhealthy for me, that it was wrong to have the priorities I'd had because I was too young. She told me not to think too much but just to accept my family as it was, like I used to; not to try to love them less but to concentrate on other things like school and my friends and things like plays (Mum got me into this summer school Mr Rossy ran, that produced a play – not even a musical; it was this terrific play called *Inherit the Wind* – though he looked at me nervously all the time as if I was a rescued wild monkey that might jump onto his head). And boys. I didn't say fat chance, because we'd already talked about those issues.

I think Social Services insisted on the counselling, but I'm sure Mum and Dad would have been all over it anyway. They got some too, actually. I suppose it probably helped. Them getting back together just at that time must have been pretty intense, but they seemed all right; they even stopped looking at us with all that concern in the end, but you could still see them being careful. They stopped telling us some stuff. They said we had to try and take a step back and trust adults. We were meant to take a step back from Iris too, not to stop caring about her but to try and see her as a sister, instead of the way we had been thinking of her.

Of course it wasn't as easy as that. I couldn't stop worrying about her just because I wasn't in charge anymore. For a long time I couldn't unknit the knot in my stomach when I thought about her being taken away from us. I still get it, though it's smaller, every time Leanne comes round. She doesn't come often but it's often enough for me, even though she says she's coming to see Mum, not Iris.

The other thing that happened not long after it all went bust was that we found out we were going to lose Feng. Mum told us that his mother had been getting ready to have him for ages, but she just hadn't felt able to make that last step and ask for him back. I don't know what tipped her over the edge, if it was being angry with us for dragging Feng into things like we had, or being angry with Mum and Dad for not keeping more of an eye on us, or feeling that anyone, even her, could look after kids better than we'd all managed. Mum said she didn't think it was exactly any of those, but that anyway it wasn't something to feel guilty about because it was a good thing. So there it was. We were only just getting used to having the baby in the house and now Feng was going.

Even after all the counselling we didn't know how to talk about it properly. I didn't want to make it any harder for Feng than it might have been already by saying that I was upset. 'Are you glad?' I did ask him once, after it was all settled.

'I'm glad but I'm also sad,' he said. Feng never found it as hard to clarify his feelings as the rest of us.

'I'm sad,' I managed, 'but I'm also glad. For you, I mean.' We left it at that really, and I felt totally inadequate.

Then, the night before his mum was coming to get him, I was awake. I'd heard Iris complaining, and even though Mum and Dad always looked after her in the night now, I couldn't go back to sleep. I got up to go to the bathroom and I heard Feng crying in his room. I went and got into bed with him, and we talked. It was easier than usual, I suppose because it was dark.

Mum heard us then – she'd developed ears like the BFG since we had Iris – and came and sat on Feng's bed and asked us how we were feeling. There was an awful lot of asking about feelings in those days, there still is. Feng told her, and we all had a bit of a cry together. Then she said, 'What about you, Phoebe?'

It really was dark, being the middle of the night and not midsummer anymore. I tried to tell them how I was feeling, about how there was this underneath layer of feeling, still, that was strong and heavy, and even when it

243

was mostly a happy feeling there was worry and pain in it. And then there was this other set of feelings on top that were more normal and easy but could still be intense. And how the sad feelings I had about Feng leaving were all running through the layers, although I was happy for him, and his mum too. And how I was worried that the way I'd been thinking just for a couple of days about how we really all felt like a family now was going to go away.

Mum was quiet for a long time beside me. I could hear her breathing in the dark. Then she said, 'You're trying to describe motherhood, Phoebe. Or, I should say,' she said, turning her face towards Feng, 'parenthood.'

I miss Feng still. We don't see him very often because he lives quite a long way away, and it's not easy us all going anywhere. He seems happy when we do see him, though it's always a bit awkward. He's not part of our family anymore, though he's still part of the family we were. I keep a picture of him and Iris, from that day in the garden, in my bedroom; I often look at those photos.

We haven't had any more kids to foster. I've never asked if we're not allowed to now because of what we did, but anyway I think we're all pretty OK with things the way they are. Mum feels guilty, like she always did, while there are children out there who need help, but she's got her hands full and she says she's trying to accept that she can't help everyone.

We're all pretty busy with other things too. Adam isn't as feverish as he used to be with all his activities – he doesn't visit the old people anymore because he says he hates them, and he doesn't swim anywhere near as much. He went back to chess club instead, and joined the film club and the history of art group at school too. He says he's come to terms with what he's actually interested in. I'm doing better in school, I'm in all the plays when they come up, and I spend a lot of time with my friends – the old ones and the new ones. Sometimes when I've got nothing better to do I go round to Kiran's house and listen to his music. I'm teaching Cal to read too, or trying to; he's no better at sitting still.

I worry still too, though my heart's calmed down a bit and I'm able to pay some attention to other things. Lily says she can still tell when I start thinking about home at school, but she says it's a good sign that now it mostly happens in chemistry or French. I worry about Cal, who's crazy sometimes and who sometimes gets upset and thinks he's going to be sent away. I worry about Mum and Dad, though they're getting on great these days; and Adam who doesn't mind being a geek anymore but still spends a lot of time in the shed. But it's mostly Iris I worry about. Even when I'm not thinking about Leanne, there are the things that can happen to any child, or anyone. She's just about walking now – she totters about between us from one pair of arms to another, and I worry that she'll just walk under a car one day, or off a pier or towards the wrong person. But it's a long time till she's grown up, and even then bad things can happen, so I'm just going to have to get used to it. I can't keep her safe, no one can. Mum says that's growing up, realising things like that, and she's still doing it herself. You've got to learn when to hold on and when to let go, and when to have your arms stretched out, just in case.

Acknowledgements

I would like to thank the British Association of Adoption and Fostering for their advice and encouragement at an early stage of this book. Any mistakes or inaccuracies are entirely my own work.

Huge thanks go to my agent, Robert Caskie, who has been altogether a class act. Also to Ruth Knowles and Eloise Wilson for picking out this book and making it so much better.

Thank you to Rebecca Gowland who cheered me up on a bad morning when she told me she'd cried over a sentence I wrote; and has had quite the hand in how all this has worked out so far – also to Jasper Hadman and Lucy Dundas.

Thank you, Mum and Dad and Conal and Anna who brought me up to have self-confidence and self-doubt in such spades. I sound like Cordelia – I mean I love you all.

Immense love and thanks to my husband, Pete, for the boundless support he gives me in every way, and without whom my life and work would both be infinitely more rubbish; to Oscar and to Aobh for being my heroes; and to Jeff, who was the baby in this book.

Abela

BERLIE DOHERTY

Two girls.

Abela lives in an African village and has lost everything. What will be her fate as an illegal immigrant? Will she find a family in time?

'I don't want a sister or brother,' thinks Rosa in England. Could these two girls ever become sisters?

Abela is the powerful and moving story of a true heroine who overcomes great hardship. Double Carnegie-winning author Berlie Doherty writing at her very best.

Shortlisted for the Manchester Book Award, the Coventry Inspiration Book Award 2009 and The Blue Peter Book Awards.

'Excellent . . . what could be an unbearably sad tale is made compulsively readable by a writer of grace and skill.' *Independent*

HBK 9781842706893 £10.99
PBK 9781842707258 £5.99

The Baby and Fly Pie
MELVIN BURGESS

'Gritty and realistic . . . Can't be put down'
Books for Keeps

'*We're the rubbish kids, losers and orphans. Every day
we go out on to the Tip to sort rubbish for Mother
Shelly.*'

For Sham, Fly Pie and his sister Jane, this is the
grim reality of their lives. Then one day everything
changes when they find a baby on the Tip –
a baby worth seventeen
million pounds . . .

This discovery takes them into
a savage, lonely city and so
begins an endless fight for
survival.

9781849394550 £5.99

When You Reach Me

REBECCA STEAD

Miranda's life is starting to unravel. Her best friend, Sal, gets punched by a kid on the street for what seems like no reason, and he shuts Miranda out of his life. Then the key Miranda's mum keeps hidden for emergencies is stolen, and a mysterious note arrives:

'I am coming to save your friend's life, and my own. I ask two favours. First, you must write me a letter.'

The notes keep coming, and whoever is leaving them knows things no one should know. Each message brings her closer to believing that only she can prevent a tragic death. Until the final note makes her think she's too late.

Winner of the John Newbery Medal 2010

Shortlisted for the Waterstone's Children's Book Prize

'Smart and mesmerising'
New York Times

9781849392129 £6.99